To Mum, Dad and the whole family,
with love and thanks

The Growing Pains of

ADRIAN MOLE

SUE TOWNSEND

Mammoth

The line drawings in the text are by Caroline Holden

First published in 1984
Methuen Paperback edition published in 1985
First published 1989 by Mammoth
an imprint of Reed International Books Ltd
Michelin House, 81 Fulham Road, London SW3 6RB
and Auckland, Melbourne, Singapore and Toronto
Reprinted 1989, 1990 (three times), 1991 (twice), 1992 (twice),
1993 (twice), 1994 (twice), 1995 (twice)

Mandarin is an imprint of Reed International Books Ltd

Copyright © 1984 Sue Townsend
Drawings copyright © 1984 Caroline Holden

ISBN 0 7497 0101 3

A CIP catalogue record for this title
is available from the British Library

Printed and bound in Great Britain by
BPC Paperbacks Ltd
A member of
The British Printing Company Ltd

The Growing Pains of Adrian Mole

The first volume of Adrian Mole's diary took him to his fifteenth birthday and a humiliating accident to his nose with a model aeroplane and some glue. This new book takes up where the previous diary left off....

Sunday May 9th: I have just realized that I have never seen a dead body or a real female nipple. This is what comes of living in a cul-de-sac.

Thursday July 1st: Nigel has arranged for me to have a blind date with Sharon Botts. I am meeting her at the roller-skating rink on Saturday. I am dead nervous. I don't know how to roller-skate, let alone make love.

Life in the Mole family is turbulent and full of surprises. As Adrian comments on New Year's Eve, 'If my father announced that he was really a Russian agent or my mother ran away with a circus knife-thrower I wouldn't raise an eyebrow....'

'Written with great verve, and showing an uncanny understanding of the young, Sue Townsend holds the balance between innocence and precocity and the result is both hilarious and salutary.'
Daily Telegraph

'The new book takes up the diary where the last left off, and is quite as classic.' *Financial Times*

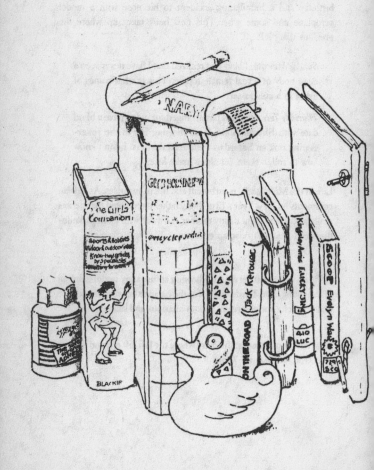

longer a Christian believer. She'll just have to find somebody else to help her up the hill to the church. Didn't get an Easter egg: my mother and father said I am too old. Anybody would think there is a law against people of fifteen eating Easter eggs!

Monday   April 12th
EASTER MONDAY

I think mother is cracking up; she is behaving even more strangely than usual. She came into my bedroom to change my sheets and when I objected to her dropping cigarette ash on my Falklands Campaign map she said, 'For God's sake, Adrian, this room is like a bloody shrine! Why don't you leave your clothes on the floor like *normal* teenagers?'

I said that I like things to be neat and tidy but she said, 'You're a bloody obsessive,' and went out.

My mother and father are always arguing about their bedroom. My father's side of the room is dead neat, but my mother's side is disgusting: overflowing ashtrays, old yellow *Observer*s, books, magazines and puddles of nylon knickers on the floor. *Her* bedside shelves are full of the yukky junk she buys from second-hand shops, one-armed statues, broken vases and stinking old books etc. I pity my father having to share a room with her. All *he's* got on his shelves are his AA book and a photograph of my mother in a wedding dress. She's the only bride I've seen who's got cigarette smoke coming out of her nostrils.

I just can't understand why my father married her.

Tuesday   April 13th

After *Crossroads* had finished I asked my father why he had married my mother. Talk about opening the floodgates! Fifteen years of bitterness and resentment spilled out. He said, 'Never make the mistake I made, Adrian. Don't let a woman's body blind you to her character and habits.'

He explained that he met my mother when miniskirts were in fashion. He said that in those days my mother had superb legs and thighs. He said, 'You must realize that most women looked bloody awful in miniskirts, so your mother had a certain rarity value.'

I was shocked at his sexist attitude and told him that I was in love with Pandora because of her brains and compassion for lesser mortals. My father gave a nasty laugh and said, 'Oh yeah! And if Pandora was as ugly as sin you wouldn't have noticed her bloody IQ and bleeding heart in the first place.'

He ended our first man-to-man talk by saying, 'Look, kiddo, don't even think about getting married until you've spent a few months sharing a bedroom with a bird. If she leaves her knickers on the floor for more than three days running forget it!'

Wednesday   April 14th

Mitzi's owner came round to ask my mother to keep our dog away from Mitzi. My mother said that the dog lived in a liberal household and was allowed to go where it pleased.

Mitzi's owner, a Mrs Carmichael, said that if our dog 'continued harassing Mitzi' she would be forced to report our dog to the police. My mother laughed and said, 'Why don't you go the whole hog and take a High Court injunction out?'

Mr Carmichael came round half an hour later. He said that Mitzi was being prepared for Crufts and mustn't suffer any stress. My mother said, 'I've got better things to do than to stand here talking about a romance between a bloody cocker spaniel and a mongrel.' I hoped this would mean she would cook some dinner but no, she went into the kitchen and read *The Guardian* from cover to cover, so I opened a tin of tuna again.

Thursday   April 15th

Woke up at 4 a.m. with a toothache. Took six junior aspirins for the pain. At 5 a.m. I woke my mother and father and told them that I was in torment.

My father said, 'It's your own bloody fault for missing your last three dentist's appointments.'

At 5.30 a.m. I asked my father to drive me to the hospital Casualty Department, but he refused and turned over in bed. It's all right for him: he hasn't got any real teeth. I sat up, racked with agony, and watched the sky get light. The lucky toothless birds started their horrible squawking and I swore that from this day forward I would go to the dentist's four times a year, whether I was in pain or not.

At nine o'clock my mother woke me up to tell me that she'd made me an appointment at the dentist's emergency clinic. I told her that the pain had stopped and instructed her to cancel the appointment.

Friday   April 16th
MOON'S LAST QUARTER

Woke up at 3 a.m. in agony with toothache. I tried to suffer in silence but my pain-racked sobs must have filtered through to my parents' bedroom because my father crashed into my room and asked me to be quiet. He showed no sympathy, just moaned on about how he had to work on the canal tomorrow and he needed his sleep. On his way back to bed he slipped on one of my mother's *Cosmopolitan*s that she'd left on her side of the bedroom floor. His swearing woke the dog up. Then my mother woke up. Then the lousy birds started. So once again I watched dawn's grey fingers infiltrate the night.

Saturday   April 17th

Still in bed with toothache.

My parents are showing me no sympathy, they keep saying, 'You should have gone to the dentist's.'

I have phoned Pandora: she is coming round tomorrow. She asked me if I needed anything; I said a Mars bar would be nice. She said (quite irritably I thought), 'Heavens above, Adrian, aren't your teeth rotten enough?'

The dog has been howling outside Mitzi's gate all day. It is also off its Pedigree Chum and Winalot.

Sunday   April 18th
LOW SUNDAY

Pandora has just left my bedroom. I am just about devastated with frustration. I can't go on like this. I have written to Aunt Clara, the Agony Aunt.

> Dear Aunt Clara,
> I am a fifteen-year-old schoolboy. My grandma tells me that I am attractive and many people have commented on how mature I am for my years. I am the only child of a bad marriage (apart from the dog). My problem is this: I am deeply in love with an older girl (by three months). She is in a class above me (I don't mean in school: we are in the same class at school. I mean that she is a social class above me.) but she claims that this doesn't matter to our relationship. We have been very happy until recently when I have started to be obsessed by sex. I have fallen to self-manipulation quite a lot lately, and it is OK for a bit but it soon wears off. I know that a proper bout of lovemaking would do me good. It would improve my skin and help my mind to concentrate on my 'O' level studies.
> I have tried all sorts of erotic things, but my girl-friend refuses to go the whole hog. She says we are not ready.
> I am quite aware of the awesome things about bringing an unwanted baby into the world and I would wear a protective dildo.
> > Yours in desperation,
> > Poet of the Midlands

Monday   April 19th

We had a dead good debate in Social Studies this morning. It was about the Falklands.

Pandora put the proposition 'That this class is against the use of force to regain the Falkland Islands.'

The standard of debate was quite good for a change. I made a brilliant speech in favour of the motion. I quoted from *Animal*

Farm and *The Grapes of Wrath*. I got quite a good round of applause when I sat down.

Barry Kent spoke *against* the proposition. He said, 'Er, I er, fink we should er, you know, like, bomb the coast of Argentina.' He was quoting from his father, yet *he* sat down to a standing ovation!

Dentist's at 2.30, worse luck!

4 p.m. I am now minus a front tooth! The stupid Australian dentist took it *out* instead of repairing it. He even had the nerve to wrap it in a bit of tissue paper and give it to me to take home!

I said, 'But I've got a gap!' He said, 'So has Watford, and if Watford can get used to it so can you.'

I asked him if another tooth would grow in its place. He said, 'Bloody ignorant Poms,' under his breath, but he didn't answer my question.

As I was stumbling out of his surgery clutching my frozen-up jaw he said that he had often seen me walking home from school eating a Mars bar, and it would be entirely my own fault if I was toothless at thirty.

I will walk home another way in future.

Tuesday   April 20th

I have now got the kind of face that you see on 'Wanted' posters. I look like a mass murderer. My mother is dead mad with the dentist; she has written him a letter demanding that he makes a false tooth free of charge.

School was terrible; Barry Kent started calling me 'Gappy Mole' and soon everyone was at it; even Pandora was a bit distant. I sent her a note in Physics asking her if she still loved me. She sent a note back saying, 'I will love you for as long as Britain has Gibraltar.'

Wednesday   April 21st

It has just been on the news that Spain wants Gibraltar back.

Thursday   April 22nd

I couldn't face taking my gap to school this morning so I stayed in bed until 12.45 p.m. I asked my mother for an excuse note. I gave it to Ms Fossington-Gore during afternoon registration. She read it angrily then said, 'At least your mother is honest. It makes a change from the usual lies one has come to expect from most parents.'

She showed me the letter. It said:

> Dear Ms Fossington-Gore,
> Adrian did not come to school this morning because he didn't get out of bed until 12.45.
> Yours faithfully,
> Ms Pauline Mole

I will get my father to write my excuse notes in future; he is a born liar.

Friday   April 23rd
ST GEORGE'S DAY (ENGLAND). NEW MOON

Barry Kent came to school in a Union Jack tee-shirt today. Ms Fossington-Gore sent him home to change. Barry Kent shouted, 'I'm celebratin' our patron saint's birthday ain't I?'

Ms Fossington-Gore shouted back, 'You're wearing a symbol of fascism, you nasty NF lout.'

Today is also Shakespeare's birthday. One day I will be a great writer like him. I am well on the way: I have already had two rejection letters from the BBC.

Saturday   April 24th

Barry Kent's father is on the front of the local paper tonight. He is pictured holding Barry Kent's Union Jack tee-shirt. The caption underneath his picture says: 'A Patriot mourns loss of National Pride.'

The article said:

> Burly World War Two veteran Frederick Keñt (45) spoke to our reporter in his homely Council house

lounge about his profound feelings of regret that his son Barry (15) was ridiculed and humiliated because he wore a Union Jack tee-shirt to school. Barry is a pupil at Neil Armstrong Comprehensive School. Mrs Kent (35) said, 'My son Barry is a sensitive boy who worships his country and is very fond of St George, so he wore a tee-shirt what had a picture of our great English flag.' Mr Frederick Kent interjected, 'On account of how it was St. George's birthday yesterday.'

Mr Kent is refusing to let his son attend school until the teacher concerned, Ms Fossington-Gore (31), makes a public apology.

Mr Reginald Scruton (57), headmaster of the school, said on the telephone today: 'I know the wretched Kent family only too well and I'm sure that we can work something out so that it doesn't make the local rag.' When it was pointed out to Mr Scruton that he was in fact talking to Roger Greenhill, our Education correspondent, Mr Scruton apologized and made the following statement: 'No comment.'

Sunday   April 25th
SECOND AFTER EASTER.
DAYLIGHT SAVING TIME BEGINS (USA AND CANADA)

British troops have recaptured South Georgia. I have adjusted my campaign map accordingly.

Found a strange device in the bathroom this morning. It looked like an egg timer. It said 'Predictor' on the side of the box. I hope my mother is not dabbling with the occult.

Monday   April 26th

A mysterious conversation! My mother said, 'George it's positive.' My father said, 'Christ, I can't go through all that three o'clock in the morning stuff again, not at my age.'

It sounds as if my mother is making unreasonable sexual demands on my father.

Tuesday   April 27th

Got a letter from Aunt Clara! I read it on the way to school.

> Dear Poet of the Midlands,
> Well, well, well, you are in a lather aren't you, lovey!
> Look, you're fifteen, your body's in a whirl, your
> hormones are in a maelstrom. Your emotions are up and
> down like a yo-yo.
>
> And of course you want sex. Every lad of your age
> does. But, my dear, there are people who crave
> penthouse apartments and exotic holidays. We can't have
> what we want all the time.
>
> You sound as if you've got a nice sensible lassie; enjoy
> each other's company. Take up a hobby, keep physically
> and mentally alert and learn to control your breathing.
>
> Sex is only a small part of life, my dear lad. Enjoy your
> precious teenage years.
> > Sincerely,
> > Aunt Clara

Enjoy my precious teenage years! They are nothing but
trouble and misery. I can't wait until I am fully mature and can
make urban conversation with intellectuals.

Wednesday   April 28th

Stick Insect (alias Doreen Slater) called round to our house
today. I haven't seen her since my father and her broke it off.

She was breathing dead quickly and she had a funny look in
her eyes. When my father came to the door she didn't say
anything, she just opened her coat (she's put a bit of weight on)
and said, 'I thought you ought to know, George,' and turned
and went down the garden path.

My father didn't say anything. He just leaned against the
bannisters sort of weakly.

I said, 'She's looking well isn't she?'

My father muttered, 'Blooming,' then he put his coat on and
went to catch her up.

Five minutes later my mother came back from her Jane Fonda's robot class at the neighbourhood centre, she was dead pleased because she had broken the pain barrier.

She shouted, 'George,' looked in all the rooms, then asked, 'When did you last see your father?'

I kept quiet, like the kid in the painting. My mother goes berserk if anyone mentions Stick Insect's name.

Thursday   April 29th

School is dead brilliant now that Barry Kent's shaved head and ferocious boots are but a bad memory.

Went to the dentist's for an impression. He called me 'Matilda'. I was unable to object because my mouth was full of putty.

Friday   April 30th
MOON'S FIRST QUARTER

My mother and father are getting through a bottle of Vodka a week. Not a minute goes by without one or the other of them bashing the ice tray or slicing a lemon or running to the off-licence for Schweppes.

This is a bad sign. It means something is going to happen.

Saturday   May 1st

Grandma rang with her annual gibberish about 'Cast ne'er a clout'. I know it's got something to do with keeping your vest on. But so what? I keep my vest on all the year round anyway.

Britain has bombed Port Stanley airport and put it out of action.

Sunday   May 2nd
THIRD AFTER EASTER

Went round to Nigel's and was astounded to hear that his parents are trying to emigrate to Australia! How could any

English person want to live abroad? Foreigners can't help living abroad because they were born there, but for an English person to go is ridiculous, especially now that sun-tan lamps are so readily available.

Nigel agrees with me. He asked me if he could stay behind and live at our house. I warned him about the poor standard of living but he said he would bring all his consumer durables with him.

Monday   May 3rd
MAY DAY HOLIDAY (UK EXCEPT SCOTLAND)
BANK HOLIDAY (SCOTLAND)

This morning I spent half an hour in the bathroom studying my nose, after my so-called best friend Nigel asked me last night if I realized I was a Dustin Hoffman look-alike.

I hadn't realized that my nose had grown to such an abnormal size. But the more I looked at it the more I could see that it *is* huge.

My mother bashed on the door and shouted, 'Whatever you're doing in there, stop it at once and come down and eat your breakfast. Your cornflakes are getting soggy!'

When I got downstairs I asked my mother if I reminded her of Dustin Hoffman. She said, 'You should be so lucky, dearie.'

Tuesday   May 4th

My mother has stopped wearing a bra. Her bust looks like two poached eggs that have been cooked for too long. I wish she wouldn't wear such tight tee-shirts. It's not dignified in somebody her age (37).

Wednesday   May 5th

A strange phone call. The phone rang and I picked it up but before I could say our number a posh woman said: 'Clinic here. You have an appointment with us on Friday at 2 p.m. Will you be able to keep the appointment, Mrs Mole?'

I said, 'Yes,' in a falsetto voice.

'You will be with us for two hours, during that time you will see two doctors and a counsellor who is very experienced in your particular problem,' she said mechanically.

I said, 'Thank you,' in a high-pitched squeak.

She went on, 'Please bring a sample of urine with you, a *small* sample, no full-to-the-brim pickle jars, please.'

'All right,' I croaked.

'Don't upset yourself, Mrs Mole,' the woman said slushily. 'We are here to help, you know.' Then she said, 'Please don't forget our fee. It will be forty-two pounds for your initial consultation.'

'No,' I whispered.

'So Friday at 2 o'clock. Please be punctual.' Then she put the phone down.

What does it all mean? My mother has not said anything about being ill. What is her particular problem? Which 'clinic'?

Thursday   May 6th

I heard some very yukky woman talking on Radio Four tonight about how she became a millionairess from writing romantic fiction books. She said that women readers like books about doctors and electronics wizards and people like that. I am going to have a go myself. I could do with a million pounds. The woman said it is important for an author of romantic fiction to have an evocative name, so, after much thought, I have decided to call myself Adrienne Storme. I have already written half the first page:

> *Longing for Wolverhampton by Adrienne Storme*
> Jason Westmoreland's copper-flecked eyes glanced cynically around the terrace. He was sick of Capri and longed for Wolverhampton.
>   He flexed his remaining fingers and examined them ꞏritically. The accident with the chain saw had ended his brilliant career in electronics. His days were now devoid of microchips. There was a yawning chasm in his life. He

had tried to fill it with travel and self-gratification but nothing could blot out the memories he had of Gardenia Fetherington, the virginal plastic surgeon at St Bupa's in Wolverhampton.

Jason brooded, blindly blinking back big blurry tears. . . .

Friday   May 7th

My mother and father were having a discussion about feminism in the car on the way to Sainsbury's this evening. My father said that since my mother's consciousness had been raised he had noticed that she had lost two inches round her bust.

My mother said angrily, 'What have my breasts got to do with anything?' There was a silence then she said, 'But don't you think I have grown as a person, George?'

My father said, 'On the contrary, Pauline, you are much smaller since you stopped wearing high heels.'

Me and my father laughed quite a lot but not for long because my mother gave us one of her powerful glances, then she looked out of the car window. She had a few tears in her eyes.

She looked at me and said, 'If only I had a daughter to talk to.'

My father said, 'We can't take the risk of having another baby like Adrian, Pauline.' Then they began to talk about my babyhood. They made me sound like Damian in the film of *The Omen*.

My mother said, 'It's that bloody Dr Spock's fault that Adrian has turned out like he has.'

I said, 'What *have* I turned out like?'

My mother said, 'You're an anal retentive, aren't you?' and my father said, 'You're tight-fisted, and you've always got your perfectly groomed head in a book.'

I was so shocked I couldn't speak for a bit but, trying to keep my voice light and melodious (not easy when your heart is pierced with the arrows of criticism), I said, 'What sort of son did you want then?'

Their answer took us all around Sainsbury's, through the queue at the checkout, and back to the multi-storey car park.

My father's ideal son was a natural athlete, he was cheerful and outgoing, he was a fluent linguist, he was tall with ruddy unblemished cheeks, he took his hat off to ladies. He went fishing with his father and swapped jokes. He was good with his hands and had a hobby making grandfather clocks. He was good officer material. He would vote Conservative and would marry into a good family. He would set up his own computer business in Guildford.

However, my mother's ideal son would be intense and saturnine. He would go to a school for the Intellectually Precocious. He would fascinate girls and women at an early age, he would enthral visitors with his witty conversation. He would wear his clothes with panache, he would be completely non-sexist, non-agist, non-racist. (His best friend would be an old African woman.) He would win a scholarship to Oxford, he would take the place by storm and be written about in future biographies. Her would turn down offers of safe parliamentary seats in Britain. Instead, he would go to South Africa and lead the blacks into a successful revolution. He would return to England where he would be the first man deemed fit to edit *Spare Rib*. He would move in sparkling social circles. He would take his mother everywhere he went.

When they'd both finished spouting on I said, 'Well I'm sorry if I'm a disappointment to you.'

My mother said, 'It's not your fault, Adrian, it's ours, we should have called you BRETT!!!'

Saturday   May 8th
FULL MOON

I needed to talk to somebody about my sense of inferiority (which grew even bigger in the night as I lay awake and thought about Brett Mole, the phantom son). So I went to Grandma's.

She showed me my baby photos. I must admit that I *was* a bit grotesque: I was completely bald until I was two and I always had a dead fierce expression on my face. Now I know why my mother hasn't got a Technicolor gilt-framed photograph of me on top of our television like other mothers.

But I'm glad I went to Grandma's; she thinks everything about me is brilliant. I told her about Brett Mole, the boy that never was. She said, 'He sounds a right nasty piece of work to me. I'm glad you didn't turn out like *him*.'

Grandma had a bit of arthritis in her shoulder so she took her dress off and I sprayed Ralgex on the pain. Grandma's corset looks like a parachute harness. I asked her how she gets in and out of it. She told me it was all down to self-discipline. She has got a theory that since corsets went out of fashion England has lost its backbone.

Sunday   May 9th
4TH AFTER EASTER. MOTHER'S DAY (USA AND CANADA)

I have just realized that I have never seen a dead body or a real female nipple. This is what comes of living in a cul-de-sac.

Monday   May 10th

I asked Pandora to show me one of her nipples but she refused. I tried to explain that it was in the interests of widening my life experience, but she buttoned her cardigan up to the neck and went home.

Tuesday   May 11th

We did diabetes in human biology today. Mr Dooher taught us to measure our blood sugar level by testing our wee. This reminded me that I forgot to tell my mother about her appointment at the clinic. Still, I don't suppose it was important.

Wednesday   May 12th

I received the following letter from Pandora this morning:

> Adrian,
> I am writing to terminate our relationship. Our love was once a spiritual thing. We were united in our appreciation of art and literature, but Adrian you have changed. You have become morbidly fixated with my body. Your request to look at my left nipple last night finally convinced me that we must part.
>   Do not contact me,
>   Pandora Braithwaite
> P.S. If I were you I would seek professional psychiatric help for your hypochondria and your sex mania. Anthony Perkins, who played the maniac in *Psycho* was in analysis for ten years, so there is no need to be ashamed.

Thursday · May 13th

Yesterday before I opened *that* letter I was a normal type of intellectual teenager. Today I know what it is to suffer. I am now an adult. I am no longer young. In fact I have noticed wrinkles forming on my forehead. I wouldn't be surprised if my hair doesn't turn white overnight.

I am in total anguish!
I love her!
I love her!
I love her!
Oh God!
Oh Pandora!

3 a.m. I have used a whole Andrex toilet roll to mop up my tears. I haven't cried so much since the wind blew my candy floss away at Cleethorpes.

2 a.m. I slept fitfully, then got out of bed to watch the dawn break. The world is no longer exciting and colourful. It is grey and full of heartbreak. I thought of doing myself in, but it's not really fair on the people you leave behind. It would upset my mother to come into my room and find my corpse. I shan't bother doing my 'O' levels. I'll be an intellectual road sweeper. I will surprise litter louts by quoting Kafka as they pass me by.

Friday   May 14th

Why oh why did I ask Pandora to show me *her* nipple? Anybody's nipple would have done. Nigel says that Sharon Botts will show *everything* for 50p and a pound of grapes.

I have written Pandora a short note.

> Pandora Darling,
> What can I say? I was crude and clumsy and should have known you would run from me like a startled faun.
>   Please, at least grant me an audience and let me apologize in person.
>   Yours with unvanquished love,
>   Adrian

I think it hits the right note. I got the 'startled faun' bit from one of Grandma's yukky romantic novels. I have sprayed a bit of my mother's 'Tramp' perfume on to the envelope and I will deliver it by hand after dark tonight.

Tramp! Fancy calling a perfume *Tramp*! Ha! Ha! Ha!

Saturday   May 15th
SCOTTISH QUARTER DAY

There were a lot of visitors at Pandora's house. I could hardly get up the drive for Jaguars and Rovers and Volvos. At first I thought there had been a death in the family because I could see two nuns and a priest eating sausage rolls in the kitchen. Then a gorilla walked in and took a bottle of wine out of the fridge so I realized it must be a fancy dress party. I hid behind the summer house so that I could get a better view: there was a cowboy and a devil talking in one bedroom and a frogman and three gipsies laughing in another. A knight in armour was clanking about in the garden. He was being followed by a cavewoman who was shouting, 'Stand still, Damian. I've found a tin opener!'

Assorted fairies and Kermits and clowns were dancing downstairs, then the gorilla burst in and started dancing with a belly dancer who was wearing a most disgusting flimsy costume which showed her navel and most of her nipples. The belly dancer kept her yashmak on which I thought was hypocritical – as if anybody was interested in looking at her face!

I couldn't see Pandora anywhere, so after about half an hour I ran up to the door and put my letter through the letterbox. As I turned to run back down the drive Toulouse Lautrec shuffled out and was sick in one of the bay tree tubs.

I got home to find Queen Victoria and Prince Albert in our kitchen. Queen Victoria said, 'We're going to the Braithwaites'.' Prince Albert said, 'The dog needs feeding.' Then they swept regally out of the kitchen and up the road to Pandora's. Nobody tells me anything in this house.

Sunday May 16th
ROGATION SUNDAY. MOON'S LAST QUARTER

3 p.m. My mother keeps being sick. It serves her right for staying out until 4 a.m. drinking. My father is still in bed, but he will have to get up soon. He has promised to take Grandma to the garden centre after tea.

7 p.m. Garden centres must be the most boring places on earth, yet adults walk around them with expressions of ecstasy on their faces!

My grandma bought a dozen rose sticks and a bag of fertilizer and a plastic Cupid urn.

My father bought a rose stick called 'Pauline'. He and my mother looked at each other in a sloppy sort of way and held hands over the stick. I left them to it and went and looked at the poisons on the bottom shelves.

I was toying with the idea of buying a bottle when Grandma shouted and asked me to come and carry the fertilizer to the car. Thus my mind was torn from thoughts of death.

Monday   May 17th

I was doing my maths homework in the fourth years' cloakroom when I overheard Pandora's confident voice ringing out.

'Yes it *was* a brillo party. But, my dear, I'm rather worried.'

Claire Neilson said, 'Why's that, Pan?'

Pandora said seriously, 'I so *enjoyed* dressing up as a belly dancer, even though it's quite against my feminist principles to exhibit my body.'

Then they moved away down the corridor gassing about Claire Neilson's cat who is expecting kittens.

So, Pandora, who refused to show me *one* of her nipples in the privacy of my bedroom is quite prepared to flaunt *both* nipples at a mixed gathering!!!

Tuesday   May 18th

Bumped into Stick Insect in the library. She had her son, Maxwell House, with her. For a thin woman she certainly looked fat.

Maxwell chucked books off the shelves while Stick Insect and I talked about the days when she had been my father's girl-friend. I told her that she had had a lucky escape from my father, but she defended him, saying, 'He is another person when he is on his own with me. He is so sweet and kind.' Yes, and so was Dr Jekyll.

Got *The Condition of the Working Class in England* by Frederick Engels out of the library.

10.30 p.m. I have just realized that Stick Insect used the present tense when she was referring to her relationship with my father. It is absolutely disgraceful. A woman of thirty not knowing the fundamentals of grammar!

Wednesday   May 19th

No word from Pandora. When we meet at school she looks through me as if I were the Invisible Man. I have asked Nigel where I can find Sharon Botts. I also went to the greengrocer's to find out how much grapes cost per pound.

Thursday   May 20th
ASCENSION DAY

Started reading Fred Engels' book tonight. My father saw me reading it and said, 'I don't want that Commie rubbish in my house.'

I said, 'It's about the class you came from yourself.'

My father said, 'I have worked and slaved and fought to join the middle classes, Adrian, and now I'm here I don't want my son admiring proles and revolutionaries.'

He is deluding himself if he thinks he has joined the middle classes. He still puts HP sauce on his toast.

Friday   May 21st

While I was listening to *The Archers* my mother asked me if I minded being an only child. I said on the contrary, I preferred it.

Saturday   May 22nd

My father has just asked me if I would like a sister or a brother. I said neither. Why do they keep drivelling on about kids? I hope they aren't thinking about adopting one. They are terrible parents. Look at me, I'm a complete neurotic.

Sunday   May 23rd
SUNDAY AFTER ASCENSION. NEW MOON

I couldn't sleep so I got up very early and went for a walk past Pandora's house. I thought about her lying in her Habitat bed wearing her Laura Ashley nightgown and I don't mind admitting that tears sprang to my eyes. However I dashed them away and went to call on old Bert and Queenie.

A wild old woman answered the door, she said, 'What have you got me out of bed for?' It was Queenie with her hair on end and no make-up on.

I apologized and went home to wake my parents up with a cup of tea. Were they grateful? No! My mother said, 'For God's sake, Adrian, it's cockcrow on Sunday morning. Push off and buy the papers or something.'

I bought the papers, read them, then took them up to my parents. I think the central heating must need turning down because my parents were both very red in the face. As I went out I heard my mother say, 'George, we will have to get a lock on that door.'

Monday   May 24th
VICTORIA DAY (CANADA)

Went to the youth club tonight. Barry Kent was there with his gang worse luck! Rick Lemon was showing a film about potholing in Derbyshire. I was very interested but I found it hard to concentrate on it because Barry Kent kept putting his fingers in front of the projector and making rabbits and giraffes and other animal shapes.

When Barry Kent had gone to the coffee bar to harass the Youth Work student behind the counter I told Rick Lemon about my problems. He said, 'Hey that's bad news, Adrian, but I'm busy tonight. Come and see me at 6 p.m. tomorrow night and we'll have a good rap.'

I think this means that he wants to talk to me at 6 p.m. tomorrow.

Tuesday   May 25th

Went to Rick's office in the Youth Club. We had a long talk about my problems. Rick said I was a 'typical product of the petty-bourgeoisie'. He said my problems were the result of my generation's 'alienation from an increasingly urbanized society'. He said my parents were 'morally bankrupt and spiritually dead'. He lit a long, loose herbal cigarette and said, 'Adrian, loosen up. Don't run with the herd. Try and live your life unfettered by convention.' Then he looked at his watch and said, 'Christ I told her I'd be home by seven.'

We walked outside and he got into his wobbly Citroën and said, 'You must come round for supper one night.'

I asked if he was still squatting in the old tyre factory. He said, 'No we've moved into Badger's Copse, the new Barratt housing estate.'

I can't decide if I feel better or worse after talking to Rick. On the whole I think I feel worse.

John Nott has announced on the news that 'one of our ships has been badly damaged.' I hope it is not the *Canberra*. Barry Kent's brother is on it.

Wednesday   May 26th

My mother is pregnant! My mother!!!!!!!!!!!!!!!!!

I will be the laughing stock at school. How could she do this to me? She is three months pregnant already, so in November a baby will be living in this house. I hope they don't expect me to share my room with it. There's no way I'm getting up in the night to give it its bottle.

My parents didn't prepare me or anything. We were all eating spaghetti on toast when my father said casually, 'Oh, by the way, Adrian, congratulations are in order, your mother's three months pregnant.'

Congratulations! What about my 'A' levels in two years' time? How can I study with a toddler smashing the place up around me?

10 p.m. Kissed my poor mother goodnight. She said, 'Are you pleased about the baby, Adrian?' I lied and said 'Yes.'

The ship that went down was the *Coventry*. It is very sad. I am glad that my dad got turned down by the War Office.

Thursday   May 27th

Got an airmail letter from Hamish Mancini, the American we met on holiday last year.

> 1889 West 33rd Street,
> New York

Hi there Aid!
Fazed huh! Yeah well, thought I'd communicate. Been

feelin kinda unzapped lately, guess mom's divorce to number four kinda unhinged me some. But! Hamish Mancini aint gonna stick around and take no more adult crap, no sir Aid. I'm comin over to visit you some. I got finance. I got documentation, I got nothin keepin me here. Tomorrow I get a flight and wowee I get to see your olde British cottage in the ancient Midlands region.

We'll promenade around ancient ruins. We'll explore Shakespeare land. Huh? I got me some good Lebanon.

See you Saturday buddy.

Hamish Mancini

After reading it and rereading it I think it means that Hamish Mancini is coming to stay with us on Saturday! I wish I hadn't told him that I lived in a thatched cottage.

I haven't told my parents yet. My mother said he ruined her adulterous holiday *avec* Lucas with his constant yapping.

Friday   May 28th

Dentist's after school for a false tooth fitting. He took advantage of my weak position in the dentist's chair to make disparaging remarks about British teeth. His assistant is from Malaya so they are both bitter about having lived under the Colonial jungleboot.

I walked home slowly, I was dreading breaking the news about Hamish Mancini's arrival. The dog met me halfway up the cul-de-sac. It was nice to see its happy face.

When I got in I made a big fuss over my poor pregnant mother, I made her a cup of coffee and insisted she put her feet up on the sofa. I put a cushion behind her head and gave her the *Radio Times* to read. I've seen it done in old films (Cary Grant did it to Doris Day).

My mother said, 'It's very kind of you, Adrian, but I can only sit down for a few minutes; I'm playing squash in half an hour.'

But she was in a good mood so I told her about Hamish. She rolled her eyes a bit and pulled her lips tight, but she didn't go mad. So perhaps being with child has improved her temper.

Saturday   May 29th
MOON'S FIRST QUARTER

11.30 p.m. The spare room is prepared, the pantry is full of tinned pumpkin pie, the freezer is bursting with pork grits and corn on the cob and pot roasts. The bathroom has been cleaned to American hygiene standards, the dog has been brushed but Hamish Mancini is not here.

We watched the nine o'clock news but no airliners had crashed into the Atlantic today or any other day this week.

At 11 p.m. my father said, 'Well, I'm not sitting around in my best clothes a minute longer.' So we all took our best clothes off and went to bed.

5 a.m. Hamish Mancini is in the spare room. He is playing Appalachian mountain songs on his steel guitar. He got a taxi from Heathrow Airport (130 miles!); the taxi driver found our house all right, but Hamish refused to believe that it was the right address and made the poor bloke drive round our suburb, looking for a thatched cottage. Eventually the taxi driver drove back to our house and got my father out of bed. Hamish paid the worn-out taxi driver with dollar bills.

Sunday   May 30th
WHIT SUNDAY

Hamish made a terrible *faux pas* at breakfast. He asked my mother, 'Hey, Pauline, where's that guy, Lucas?'

There was an awful silence, then my father said coldly, 'My wife and Mr Lucas are no longer friends.'

But Hamish went on! 'Gee that's too bad, Mr Lucas was cool y'know? What happened?'

My mother said, 'We don't usually talk about personal matters at breakfast, not in England,' she added.

He said, 'Wow, that great British reserve I've heard about.' He seemed really happy, as if he'd found a whole village full of thatched cottages.

In the afternoon we took him to see Bert and Queenie, he

was beside himself with joy. On the way back in the car he kept saying, 'Jee-sus! A genuine Derby [he pronounced it to rhyme with Herbie] and Joan!'

I went to bed at 10 p.m. worn out with his constant enthusiastic exclamations.

Monday   May 31st
SPRING HOLIDAY (EXCEPT SCOTLAND)
BANK HOLIDAY (SCOTLAND) MEMORIAL DAY (USA)

We took Hamish to the fun fair on our recreation ground. For once Hamish looked a bit subdued. He said, 'I guess Disneyland has kinda given me a false expectation-of-enjoyment level.'

He took my mother on the dodgems and I went on the Flying Whiplash with my father. I was dumbstruck with terror, so was my father; I was OK until I looked down and saw the moron working the machinery. He looked like a Neanderthal man in denims and I had put my life in his clumsy paws!

My father had aged ten years by the time he got off the Flying Whiplash. But when my mother asked him if he had enjoyed himself he said, 'It was grand.'

Our dog has become Hamish's devoted companion; it follows him wherever he goes. Hamish calls our dog 'ol' Blue' and sings it sickly songs about American dogs who sit on their dead masters' graves.

It makes me sick to see how easily the dog's affections are bought.

Tuesday   June 1st

Hamish wants to meet Pandora. I told him how things stand between Pandora and me, but Hamish wouldn't listen. He just said, 'But that doesn't stop *me* from meeting her, for Christ's sake.'

Grandma rang up at tea-time and asked if my father would come and collect her but I told her that we'd got an American in the house, so she said she wouldn't bother. She said, 'I'm just too old to cope with Americans, Adrian.' I know how she feels.

Hamish got Pandora's number from our pop-up phone index on the hall table, then he rang her up and invited himself round for supper!

Still, at least the house is peaceful. I am reading *The Quiet American* by Graham Greene, Hughie Greene's brother.

Wednesday   June 2nd

Hamish has gone skiing on a dry slope with Pandora. I hope they both break something, preferably their necks.

Thursday   June 3rd

I took Hamish to see how an English comprehensive school works today. The only previous knowledge he had of English schools was taken from reading *Tom Brown's Schooldays*, so Hamish was a bit disappointed to find that ritual floggings and roastings had been done away with.

Mr Dock, my English teacher, asked Hamish to give our class a short talk on 'His impressions of England.' Hamish wasn't a bit shy. He went to the front of the class, spat his chewing gum into Mr Dock's wicker basket and said, 'Well, England's great, cute, real fine. Jee-sus it's green! I mean like real green! And I just love your flues [chimneys, translated by Mr Dock]. In the Apple [New York] we don't have flues [chimneys]. I guess the coolest thing, though, is your girls. [Here his eyes met Pandora's.] They may look like icebergs on the surface, but Jee-sus the seven-eighths that's under the surface sure gets a guy warmed up.' He drivelled on for another ten minutes! I was glad when the bell rang.

It is twenty-four days since Pandora spoke to me.

Friday   June 4th

Hamish is spending every waking moment at Pandora's house. It is an abuse of our hospitality. A telegram came from

America. It was addressed to MANCINI but I opened it, in case his mother had dropped dead or something.

> BABY STOP COME HOME TO MOM STOP WE MUST TRY TO INTERACT POSITIVELY STOP HOW THE BRITS TREATING YOU STOP WIRE ME AND GIVE ME YOUR ARRIVAL AT KENNEDY STOP I GOT A NEW SHRINK STOP HE IS PORTUGUESE STOP ETHEL GLITTENSTEINER SWEARS HE CURED HER KLEPTOMANIA STOP HOW'S THE WEATHER STOP IT'S AWFUL HOT HERE STOP BUT IT IS NOT SO MUCH THE HEAT AS THE HUMIDITY STOP SAY HELLO TO ADRIAN PAULINE AND MISTER LUCAS FOR ME STOP I LOVE YOU BABY

I delivered the telegram to Pandora's house. Pandora took it from me without a word. I turned away without a word.

Saturday   June 5th

Hamish has gone home to Mom. The next time he runs away from home I hope he goes to Cape Horn or the Arctic Circle or anywhere I'm not likely to be.

Sunday   June 6th
TRINITY SUNDAY, FULL MOON

Stayed in my room all day bringing my Falklands campaign map up to date. I am very aware that I am living through a historical period and I, Adrian Mole, predict that the British People will force the government to resign.

Monday   June 7th
HOLIDAY (REPUBLIC OF IRELAND)

> My mother
> Claire Neilson's cat
> Mitzi

What have the above all got in common?

The fact that they are all expecting babies, kittens or puppies. The fecundity on this suburb is just amazing. You can't walk down the street without bumping into pregnant women and it has all happened since the council put fluoride in the water.

Tuesday   June 8th

Saw Bert Baxter outside the newsagent's. He was sitting in his wheelchair reading the *Morning Star*. We had a long talk about working-class culture. Bert said that if he were a younger man he would infiltrate into the *Sun* newspaper and smash the presses up!

He tried to get me to join the Young Communists. I said I would think about it. I thought about it for five minutes then decided not to. The GCE examiners might get to hear about it.

Wednesday   June 9th

It is time I was done with childish things so I have taken all my Enid Blyton books off my bookshelves. I have packed them into an Anchor butter box and put them outside my door. I hope my parents take the hint and stop talking to me as if I were a moron. Anyone who can understand how the International Monétary Fund works (I did it in Maths last week) deserves more respect.

Thursday   June 10th

Stick Insect is pregnant!

I saw her in the Co-op this afternoon. Maxwell House was having a tantrum at the checkout so I was spared from speaking to her. The poor woman looked dead miserable. Still it serves her right for being promiscuous. I wonder who the father is?

Friday   June 11th

My father is getting fed up with his job as a canal bank renovation supervisor. He says that no sooner do Boz, Baz,

Maz, Daz and Gaz, his gang, clear a section of canal than some slob comes along in the night and tips a month's household rubbish on the virgin bank.

The gang are getting a bit disheartened and morale is low. I offered to set up a vigilante group but my father said that anyone who has carried an old mattress 300 yards in the dark is not going to be put off dumping it by a gaggle of spotty schoolboys.

Saturday   June 12th

I have written to Mr Tydeman at the BBC and sent him another poem. I chose Norway as my theme, as I am quite an expert on the Norwegian Leather Industry.

> Dear Mr Tydeman,
> I had a few moments to spare so I thought I would pen you a letter and also send you my new poem 'Norway'. It (the poem) is in the modernist school of poetry, in other words it isn't about flowers and stuff and it doesn't rhyme. If you can't understand it, could you pass it on to someone who will explain it for you? Any modern poet will do.
>   Yours faithfully,
>   Adrian Mole (Aged 15¼)
> P.S. If you bump into Terry Wogan in the corridor could you ask him to mention my grandma on the air? Her name is May Mole and she is a seventy-six-year-old diabetic.

Norway
Norway! Land of difficult spelling.
Hiding your beauty behind strange vowels.
Land of long nights, short days and dots over 'O's.
Ruminating majestic reindeers
Tread warily on ice floes
Ever aware of what happened to the
Titanic.

One day I will sojourn to your shores
I live in the middle of England
But!
Norway! My soul resides in your watery ~~fiords fyords fiiords~~
    Inlets.

Sunday   June 13th
FIRST AFTER TRINITY

Spent the day at Grandma's reading the *News of the World* and
eating proper food for a change. We had roast lamb and mint
sauce made from the window box. Grandma is hoping that her
next grandchild is a girl. She said, 'You can dress girls nicely.'
She has already knitted a purple matinée jacket and half a pair
of bootees.

She is using neutral colours 'just in case'. I am dreading the
day when there are feet inside the bootees.

Monday   June 14th
MOON'S LAST QUARTER

Our usual postman has been replaced by another one called
Courtney Elliot. We know his name because he knocked on the
door and introduced himself. He is certainly no run-of-the-
mill postman, he wears a ruffled shirt and a red-spotted bow tie
with his grey uniform.

He invited himself into the kitchen and asked to be
introduced to the dog. When the dog had been brought in from
the back garden Courtney looked it in the eye and said, 'Hail
fellow, well met.' Don't ask me what it means; all I know is that
our dog rolled over and let Courtney tickle its belly. Courtney
refused a cup of instant coffee, saying that he only drank
fresh-ground Brazilian, then he gave my father the letters
saying, 'One from the Inland Revenue I fear, Mr Mole,' tipped
his hat to my mother and left. The letter was from the tax office.
It was to tell my father that they had 'received information' that
during the previous tax year he had been running a spice rack

construction company business from his premises, but that they had no record of such a business and so could he fill in the enclosed form? My father said, 'Some rotten sod's shopped me to the tax!' I went off to school. On the way I saw Courtney coming out of the Singhs' eating a chapati.

Tuesday   June 15th

Today Courtney brought a letter from the Customs and Excise Department. It asked my father (in very curt terms) why he hadn't registered his spice rack business for VAT.

My father shouted at the letter and said, 'Somebody's got it in for me!' My mother and father counted how many enemies they had made in their lives. It came to twenty-seven, not counting relations.

Wednesday   June 16th

My father is getting to dread Courtney Elliot's cheerful knock on our door in the morning. This morning it was a letter from Access threatening to cut my father's card in half.

I was hit on the head by a cricket ball today. It was my own fault. When I saw it coming towards me I shut my eyes and ran in the opposite direction. I am at home in bed waiting to see if concussion sets in.

Stick Insect has walked past our house six times.

Thursday   June 17th

I have just found a list at the bottom of my mother's shopping bag.

FOR IT	AGAINST IT
Might be a girl	Loss of Independence
More family allowance	George doesn't want it
	Months of looking like the side of a house
	Pain during labour
	Adrian bound to be jealous

Dog might not take to it
Am I too old at 37?
Varicose veins
PAS

Friday   June 18th

I pretended to be enthusiastic about the baby at breakfast today. I asked my mother if she had thought of any names yet. My mother said, 'Yes. I'm going to call her Christabel.'

Christabel! It sounds like somebody out of *Peter Pan*. Nobody is called Christabel. The poor kid.

Saturday   June 19th

Nigel and I went for a bike ride today. We set out to look for a wild piece of countryside so that we could get back to nature and stuff. We pedalled for miles but all the woods and fields were guarded by barbed wire and 'KEEP OUT' notices, so we could only get near to nature.

On the way back we had a philosophical discussion about war. Nigel is dead keen on it. It is his ambition to join the army. He said, 'It's a good life, and when I come back to civvy street I'll have a trade.'

I thought, 'What, as a contract killer?' But I didn't say anything. Most of the army cadets I know forget that real soldiers have to kill people.

Sunday   June 20th
SECOND AFTER TRINITY. FATHERS' DAY

My father has hogged the television for over a week, watching the lousy, stinking World Cup. This afternoon when I asked if I could watch a BBC 2 documentary about rare Norwegian plants he refused to let me switch over, and he sat in the dark watching France versus Kuwait. He was sulking because I forgot it was Fathers' Day. I made an official protest to my mother but she refused to arbitrate, so I went up to my room and brought my Falklands campaign map up to date. I also checked my Building Society account to see if I can afford a black-and-white portable. I am sick of being dependent on my parents' television set.

I went downstairs just in time to see a dead good pitch invasion led by an Arab bloke in a head-dress. I don't mind watching an interesting pitch invasion, it's the football I can't stand.

Monday   June 21st
LONGEST DAY. NEW MOON

Mr Scruton summoned the whole school into the assembly hall this morning. Even the teachers who are atheists were forced to attend.

I was dead nervous. It's ages since I broke a school rule but Scruton makes you feel dead guilty somehow. When the doors were closed and the whole school was lined up in rows Scruton nodded to Mrs Figges, who was sitting at the piano, and she started playing 'Hallelujah!'

Some of the fifth years (including Pandora) sang along using different words: 'Hallelujah! What's it to you?' etc. It was quite impressive. Though I thought it was time that the blind piano tuner called again.

When the singing stopped and Mrs Figges was still, Mr Scruton walked up to his lectern, paused, and then said, 'Today is a day that will go down in history.' He paused long enough for a rumour to travel along the rows that he was resigning, then he shouted, 'Quiet!' and continued, 'Today at three minutes to nine a future King of England was born.' All the girls, apart from Pandora, (she is a republican) said, 'Ooh! Lady Di's 'ad it!'

Claire Neilson shouted: 'How much did he weigh?'

Mr Scruton smiled and ignored her.

Pandora shouted, 'How much will he *cost*?' and Mr Scruton suddenly developed good hearing and ordered her out of the assembly hall.

Poor Pandora, her face was as red as the Russian flag as she walked along the rows to the exit door, when she passed me I tried to give her a supportive smile, but it must have come out wrong because she whispered, 'Still leering at me, Adrian?'

Mr Scruton dismissed the school after giving us a talk on what a good job the Royal Family do for British exports.

Went to bed early; it had been a long day.

Tuesday   June 22nd

The new prince left the hospital today. My father is hoping that he will be called George, after him. My mother said that it's time the Royal Family came up to date and called the Prince Brett or Jason.

Scotland are out of the World Cup. They drew 2–2 with Russia. My father called the Russian team 'those Commie bastards'. He was not a bit gracious in defeat.

Wednesday   June 23rd

Pandora has been put into isolation at school. She is working at a desk outside Scruton's office. I left the following note on her peg in the cloakroom:

> Pandora,
> A short note to say that I admired your spirited stand on Monday.
>   From Adrian Mole, your ex-lover
> P.S. My mother is with child.

Thursday   June 24th
MIDSUMMER DAY (QUARTER DAY)

Found a note on my peg at break this morning.

> Adrian,
> We were never lovers so it was inaccurate, indeed libellous, of you to sign your note 'ex-lover'. However, I thank you for your note of support.
>   Pandora

P.S. I am shocked to learn that your mother is *enceinte*.
Tell her to ring the Clinic.

Friday   June 25th

My thing is 14cm extended and about 3cm in its unwoken state.
I am dead worried. Donkey Dawkins of 5P says his thing comes
off the end of a ruler, yet he is only a week older than me.

Saturday   June 26th

It was with great pleasure that I saw Mr Roy Hattersley on
television tonight. Once again I was struck by his obvious
sincerity and good vocabulary. Mr Hattersley was predicting
that there will be an early election. He denied that Mr Michael
Foot is too scruffy to be the next Prime Minister.

Sunday   June 27th
THIRD AFTER TRINITY

I can't go on with this charade of churchgoing every Sunday. I
will have to tell Grandma that I have become an agnostic
atheist. If there *is* a God then He/She must know that I am a
hypocrite. If there isn't a God then, of course, it doesn't matter.

Monday   June 28th
MOON'S FIRST QUARTER

Bert rang me when I got home from school to bellow that Social
Services had paid for him to have a phone installed in his
pensioner's bungalow. Bert told me that he had already phoned
one of his daughters in Melbourne, Australia, and Queenie
had phoned her eldest son in Ontario, Canada. They had
listened to Dial-a-Disc, the Recipe for the Day, the Weather
Forecast, the Cricket News, and they were both looking
forward to listening to the GPO's Bedtime Story. I pointed out
to Bert that he would have to pay for each phone call he made,
but he laughed his wheezy laugh and said, 'I shall probably be a
gonner before the bill comes in.' (Bert is nearly ninety.)

Tuesday   June 29th

Usual last-minute discussion about where we are going for our summer holiday. My father said, 'It'll probably be our last. This time next year we'll have the nipper.' My mother got dead mad, she said that having a baby was not going to restrict her. She said that if she felt like walking in the Hindu Kush next year, then she would strap the baby on her back and go.

The Hindu Kush! She moans if she has to walk to the bus stop.

I suggested the Lake District. I wanted to see if living there for a bit would help my poetry.

My father suggested Skegness. My mother suggested Greece. Nobody could agree, so we each wrote our choice on a scrap of old till roll and put them into a Tupperware gravy maker. We didn't trust each other to make the draw so my mother went and fetched Mrs Singh.

Mrs Singh and all the little Singhs came and stood in our kitchen. Mrs Singh asked, 'Why are you having this procedure, Mrs Mole? Can't your husband decide?' My mother explained that Mr Mole had no superior status in our house. Mrs Singh looked shocked, but she drew a piece of paper out of the hat. It said 'Skegness'. Worse luck!

Mrs Singh excused herself, saying that she must get back to prepare her husband's meal. As she left I noticed my father glance wistfully at her in her pretty sari and jewelled sandals.

I also noticed him looking sadly at my mother in her overalls and ankle boots. My mother said, 'That poor downtrodden woman.'

My father sighed and said, 'Yes.'

Wednesday   June 30th

My mother wants to move. She wants to sell the house that I have lived in all my life. She said that we will need more room 'for the baby'. How stupid can you get? Babies hardly take any space at all. They are only about twenty-one inches long.

Thursday   July 1st
DOMINION DAY (CANADA)

Nigel has arranged for me to have a blind date with Sharon Botts. I am meeting her at the roller-skating rink on Saturday. I am dead nervous. I don't know how to roller-skate – let alone make love.

Friday   July 2nd

Borrowed Nigel's disco-skates and practised skating on the pavement in our cul-de-sac. I was OK so long as I had a privet hedge to grab at, but I dreaded skating past the open-plan gardens where there is nothing to hold on to.

I wanted to wear my skates in the house so that I would develop confidence, but my father moaned about the marks the wheels made on the cushion floor in the kitchen.

Saturday   July 3rd

12.15 p.m. Got up at 6 a.m. for more roller-skating practice. Mr O'Leary shouted abuse because of the early morning noise, so I went to the little kids' play park and practised there, but I had to give up. There was so much broken glass and dog muck lying about that I feared for the ballbearings in the skates. I waited for the greengrocer's to open, bought a pound of grapes, went home, had a bath, washed my hair and cut my toenails etc. Then I put my entire wardrobe of clothes on to the bed and tried to decide what to wear.

It was a pitiful collection. By the time I had eliminated my school uniform I was left with: three pairs of flared jeans (FLARES! Yuk! Yuk! Nobody wears flares except the worst kind of moron), two shirts, both with long pointed collars (LONG POINTS! Yuk!), four of Grandma's handknitted jumpers (HANDKNITTED! Ugh!). The only possible clothes were my bottle-green elephant cords and my khaki army sweater. But which shoes? I had left my trainers at school and I can't wear my formal wedding shoes to a roller-skating rink, can I?

At 10.30 I rang Nigel and asked him what youths wore at roller-skating rinks. He said, 'They wear red satin side vent running shorts, sleeveless satin vests, white knee socks, Sony Walkman earphones and one gold earring.' I thanked him, put the phone down and went and had another look at my clothes.

The nearest I could get were my black PE shorts, my white string vest and my grey knee socks. I am the only person in the world not to have a Sony Walkman and I haven't had my ears pierced so I couldn't manage those two items, but I hope that Sharon Bott won't mind too much.

Do I go in my shorts etc or do I change when I get to the rink? And how will I know which girl is Sharon Bott? I've only seen her in school uniform and in my experience girls are unrecognizable when they are in civilian clothes.

Must stop, it's time to go.

6 p.m. That's the first and last time I go roller-skating. Sharon Bott is an expert. She went whizzing off at 40 mph, only stopping now and again to do the splits in mid-air.

She sometimes slowed down to say, 'Let go of the barrier, Dumbo,' but she didn't stay long enough for me to divert her into having a longer conversation. When it was time for the under-twelves to monopolize the rink, she sped to the barrier and helped me into the coffee bar. We had a Coke then I clumped off to the cloakroom to get the grapes. When I gave her them she said, 'Why have you bought me grapes? I'm not poorly.' I dropped a hint by looking knowingly at her figure in its lycra body stocking and miniskirt but then the roller disco started and she sped off to do wild disco dancing on her skates. She was soon surrounded by tall skated youths in satin shorts so I staggered off to get changed.

I rang Nigel when I got home. I complained that Sharon Bott was a dead loss. He said that Sharon Bott had already rung him to complain that I had showed her up by dressing in my school PE kit.

Nigel said that he is giving up matchmaking.

Sunday July 4th

FOURTH AFTER TRINITY. AMERICAN INDEPENDENCE
DAY

I was just starting to eat my Sunday dinner when Bert Baxter rang and asked me to go round urgently. I bolted my spaghetti Bolognese down as quickly as I could and ran round to Bert's.

Sabre, the vicious Alsatian, was standing at the door looking worried. As a precaution I gave him a dog choc and hurried into the bungalow. Bert was sitting in the living room in his wheelchair, the television was switched off so I knew something serious had happened. He said, 'Queenie's had a bad turn.' I went into the tiny bedroom. Queenie was lying in the big saggy bed looking gruesome (she hadn't put her artificial cheeks or lips on). She said, 'You're a good lad to come round, Adrian.' I asked her what was wrong. She said, 'I've been having pains like red hot needles in my chest.'

Bert interrupted, 'You said the pains were like red-hot knives five minutes ago!'

'Needles, knives, who cares?' she said.

I asked Bert if he had called the doctor. He said he hadn't because Queenie was frightened of doctors. I rang my mother and asked for her advice. She said she'd come round.

While we waited for her I made a cup of tea and fed Sabre and made Bert a beetroot sandwich.

My mother and father came and took over. My mother phoned for an ambulance. It was a good job they did because while it was coming Queenie went a bit strange and started talking about ration books and stuff.

Bert held her hand and called her a 'daft old bat'.

The ambulance men were just shutting the doors when Queenie shouted out, 'Fetch me pot of rouge. I'm not going until I've got me rouge.' I ran into the bedroom and looked on the dressing table. The top was covered in pots and hair nets and hairpins and china dishes and lace mats and photos of babies and weddings. I found the rouge in a little drawer and took it to Queenie. My mother went off in the ambulance and

me and my father stayed behind to comfort Bert. Two hours
later my mother rang from the hospital to say that Queenie had
had a stroke and would be in hospital for ages.

Bert said, 'What am I going to do without my girl to help me?'

Girl! Queenie is seventy-eight.

Bert wouldn't come home with us. He is scared that the
council will take his bungalow away from him.

Monday   July 5th
INDEPENDENCE DAY HOLIDAY (USA)

Queenie can't speak. She is sort of awake but she can't move
her mouth muscles. My mother has been round at Bert's all day
cleaning and cooking. My father is going to call in every day on
his way home from the canal. I have promised to take horrible
Sabre for his morning and evening walks.

Tuesday   July 6th
FULL MOON

Bert's social worker, Katie Bell, has been to see Bert. She
wants Bert to go back into the Alderman Cooper Sunshine
Home temporarily. Bert said he 'would prefer death to that
morgue.'

Katie Bell is coming round to see us tomorrow. She is
checking Bert's lie that my mother and father and me are
providing twenty-four-hour care for him. Queenie is still very
poorly.

Wednesday   July 7th

Katie Bell is a strange woman. She talks (and looks) a bit like
Rick Lemon. She was wearing a donkey jacket and denim jeans
and she had long greasy hair parted down the middle. Her nose
is long and pointed (from poking into other people's business
my father said). She sat in our lounge rolling a cigarette in one
hand and taking notes with the other.

She said Bert was stubborn and suffering from slight senile

dementia and that what he needed was to see a consultant psychogeriatrician. My mother got dead mad and shouted, 'What he needs is a day- and a night-nurse.' Katie Bell went red and said, 'Day and night care is prohibitively expensive.'

My father asked how much it would cost to put an old person in an old people's home. Katie Bell said, 'It costs about two hundred pounds a week.'

My father shouted, 'Give me two hundred pounds a week and I'll move in and look after the old bugger.'

Katie Bell said, 'I can't relocate funds, Mr Mole.' As she was going she said, 'Look, I don't like the system any more than you do. I know it stinks, but what can I do?'

My mother said, 'You could wash your hair, dear, you'd feel much better without it straggling around your face.'

Thursday   July 8th

I left a note on Pandora's peg today. It said:

> Pandora,
> Queenie Baxter is in hospital after a stroke. Bert is on his own in the bungalow. I am going round and doing what I can, but it would be nice if you could visit him for a bit. He is dead sad. Have you got any photos of Blossom?
> > Yours, as ever,
> > Adrian

Friday   July 9th

A brilliant day today. School broke up for eight fabbo weeks. Then something *even better* happened tonight.

I was in the middle of ironing Bert's giant underpants when Pandora walked into the living room. She was carrying a jar of home-pickled beetroot. I was transfixed. She gets more beautiful every day. Bert cheered up no end. He sent me off to make some tea. I could hardly keep my hands still. I felt as if I'd had an electric shock. I looked yearningly at Pandora as I handed her her tea. And she looked yearningly back at me!!!!!!!!

We sat around looking at photos of Blossom, Pandora's ex-pony. Bert droned on about ponies and horses he had known when he was an ostler.

At 9.30 I washed Bert, sat him on the commode and then put him to bed. We sat by the electric coal fire until he started snoring, then we fell into each other's arms with little sighs and moans. We stayed like that until Bert's clock struck 10 p.m. Sex didn't cross my mind once. I just felt dead calm and comfortable.

On the way home I asked Pandora when she realized that she still loved me. She said, 'When I saw you ironing those horrible underpants. Only a superior type of youth could have done it.'

It has just been on the news that a man has been found in the Queen's bedroom. Radio Four said that the man was an intruder and was previously unknown to the Queen. My father said: 'That's her story.'

Saturday   July 10th

My father took Bert to visit Queenie, so I went to Sainsbury's on the bus. My mother gave me thirty pounds and asked me to buy enough food for five days. I remembered our last Domestic Science lesson, in which Mrs Appleyard taught us how to make cheap meals with maximum nourishment, so I bought:

    2 lb Lentils
    1 lb Dried peas
    3 lb Wholemeal flour
    1 pkt Yeast
    1 lb Castor sugar
    2 pints Plain yogurt
    20 lb King Edward's
    2 lb Brown rice
    1 lb Dried apricots
    1 Tub cream cheese
    ½ lb Krona margarine
    A large cabbage
    2 lb Breast of lamb

A huge Swede
4 lb Parsnips
2 lb Carrots
2 lb Onions

How I dragged it all to the bus stop I'll never know. The bus conductor was no help. He didn't assist me to pick a single potato from off the floor of the bus.

I am going to write and complain to Sainsbury's about their lousy brown carrier bags. They ought to stand up to being dragged half a mile without splitting. My mother didn't thank me when I handed her fifteen pounds change! She whined on and on about forgetting the frozen black forest gâteaux and tinned peas etc.

She went mad when she saw that I had not bought a white thick-sliced loaf. I pointed out that she had all the ingredients with which to make her own bread. She said, 'Correction. *You* have the ingredients!'

Spent all evening bashing dough about, then chucking it into tins. I don't know what went wrong. I opened the oven door and checked it every five minutes but it just wouldn't rise.

Sunday   June 11th
FIFTH AFTER TRINITY

Pandora says I should have kept the oven door shut.

My father refused to eat his breast of lamb stew. He went to the pub and had a microwave mince and onion pie and crinkle-cut chips.

He is asking for a coronary.

Monday   July 12th
HOLIDAY (NORTHERN IRELAND)

Brainbox Henderson has started a youth club poetry magazine. I have submitted some of my Juvenilia plus a more recent mature poem called:

Ode to Engels
or
Hymn to the Modern Poor
Engels, you catalogued the misfortunes of the poor in
    days of yore,
Little thinking that the poor would still be with us in
    nearly 1984.
Yet stay! What is this I see in 1983?
'Tis a queue of hungry persons outside the Job Centre.
Though rats and TB be but sad memories
The pushchairs of the modern poor contain pasty babies
    with hacking coughs
Young mothers draw on number six
Young fathers queue to pay fines
Old people watch life pass by the plate-glass windows of
    council homes
Oh Engels that you were still amongst us pen in hand
Your indignation a-quiver
Your fine nose tuned to the bad smells of 1983.

Pandora read it at Bert's. She says that it is a work of genius.
I have sent a copy to Bert Baxter. He is always going on about
Engels.

Tuesday   July 13th

Brainbox Henderson showed me Barry Kent's pathetic entry
for the poetry competition. Kent is convinced he is going to win
the first prize of £5. It is called 'Tulips'.

Nice, red, tall, stiff,
In a vase,
On a table,
In a room,
In our house.

According to Henderson, Kent's poem shows Japanese
cultural influences! How stupid can you get?

The nearest Barry Kent has been to Japanese culture is sitting on the pillion of a stolen Honda.

Wednesday   July 14th
MOON'S LAST QUARTER

Every night this week I have been round to Bert's and taken vile Sabre for one of his four-mile walks, but I couldn't face it tonight. I hate the way people cross the road to avoid us. Sabre hasn't bitten anybody for ages, but he always *looks as if he's about to*. Even other Alsatians flatten themselves against walls when they see Sabre approaching. I wish that Queenie would hurry up and get better; she is proud to be seen out with Sabre. She says, 'An Alsatian a day keeps the muggers at bay.'

Thursday   July 15th
ST SWITHIN'S DAY

Pandora's parents took Bert to the hospital to visit Queenie this evening, so Pandora and I spent two brillo hours lying on her parents' bed watching the video of *Rocky 1*. I kept my hands strictly away from Pandora's erotic zones. When the film finished we talked about our futures. Pandora said that after University she would like to dig water holes in the Third World countries. She demonstrated how an artesian well is sunk by using her lit cigarette. Unfortunately the cigarette fell out of her hand and burnt a hole in the duvet. Pandora is dead worried; her parents are fanatical non-smokers.

I am reading *Lucky Jim* by a bloke called Kingsley Amis. My father says that Kingsley Amis used to be the editor of the *New Statesman*. It is surprising how much my father knows about literary matters. He never reads books but he is forced to listen to Radio Four on his car radio because the dial has jammed and he can't get Terry Wogan.

Friday   July 16th
5.30 p.m. Stick Insect has just rung to ask if my father is back

from work yet. I told her that he calls in on Bert Baxter on his way home every night. She said, 'Thank you, I'll ring back later,' in a sad sort of voice. I expect she is regretting her promiscuous behaviour now that her baby is imminent.

I told my mother it was a wrong number; pregnant women should not be upset.

Saturday   July 17th

I have just seen my father and Stick Insect walking along the canal towpath arm in arm. I know the path is a bit cobbly but surely Stick Insect could have walked without assistance. It's kind of my father to support Stick Insect in her hour of need but he should be more careful of public opinion. If people see an old-looking man arm in arm with a pregnant woman they are bound to assume that he is the father of the foetus. I hid behind the old bridge until they'd passed out of sight, then went to call for Pandora.

Sunday   July 18th
SIXTH AFTER TRINITY

My father announced at breakfast that he is going to have a vasectomy. I pushed my sausages away untouched.

Monday   July 19th

Went to see Grandma after Bert's. She was making her Christmas cake. She let me drop the twenty pence pieces in the mixture and stir it around a bit while I made a wish. I was dead selfish really; I could have wished for world peace or Queenie's quick recovery or for a safe confinement for my mother, but instead I wished that the spots on my shoulders would clear up before my summer holiday. I am dreading baring my back to gawping holiday-makers on Skegness beach.

The Queen's personal detective, Commander Trestrail, has had to resign because the papers have found out that he is a homosexual. I think this is dead unfair. It's not against the law and I bet the Queen doesn't mind. Barry Kent calls *ME* a poofter because I like reading and hate sport. So I understand what it is like to be victimized.

Tuesday   July 20th
NEW MOON

Got a foreign letter, it is addressed to me but it must be a mistake. I don't know any foreigners.

> Norsk rikskringkasting, BERGEN, Norway.
> Kjaere Adrian Mole,
> John Tydeman viste meg ditt dikt 'Norge' og jeg var dypt rørt av de følelser de uttrykte. Jeg håper du en dag vil besøke vårt land. Det er vakkert og du vil kunne oppleve fjordene og se hvor Ibsen og Grieg levde. Som en intellektuell person burde det interessere deg. Når du besøker oss og snakker med oss vil du oppdage at våre vokaler ikke er så eiendommelige. Husk at vi bare har lange netter og korte dager om vinteren. I juni er det helt motsatt. Så kom om sommeren – vi skal ta imot deg på beste måte.
> Til lykke med dine studier av norsk laerindustri.
> Hjertelig hilsen
> Din,
> Knut Johansen

Wednesday   July 21st

Only eight days to go before my holiday in Skegness begins. I have asked my father if Pandora can come with us. I can't bear the thought of being alone with my parents for a fortnight. My father said, 'She's welcome to come along providing she stumps up a hundred and twenty quid.'

Thursday   July 22nd

When we were round at Bert's doing his cleaning I asked Pandora if she would like to come to Skegness. She said,

'Darling, I would follow you into Hell, but I draw the line at Skegness.'

Bert said, 'Pandora, you're nought but a stuck-up little Madam. It'll do you good to mingle with the proletariat. Life ain't all dry ski slopes and viola lessons you know.' He gave a big sigh and said, 'Personally I'd give me right ball for a week in Skeggy.'

Pandora blushed a lovely pink colour and said, 'I'm awfully sorry, Bert. One tends to forget that one's privileged.'

Bert lit a Woodbine, sighed again and said: 'I shan't 'ave another holiday now, not at my age. No: *death*'s the only rest I've got to look forward to.'

To create a diversion Pandora phoned the hospital and asked how Queenie was. The nurse said, 'Mrs Baxter asked for her pot of rouge today.' Bert cheered up when he heard this news; he said: 'That means the old gel's on the mend.' We put Bert to bed, then I walked Pandora home.

We had a dead good half-French, half-English kiss, then Pandora whispered, 'Adrian, take me to Skegness.' It was the most romantic sentence I have ever heard.

Friday   July 23rd

11 a.m. A dirty white cat turned up on our doorstep this morning. It had a tag round its neck which said, 'My name is Roy' but there was no address. It ignored me when I got the milk in so I ignored it back.

6 p.m. My mother and father have had a big row about Roy. My father accused my mother of encouraging Roy to stay by giving him (the cat) a saucer of milk. My mother accused my father of being an animal hater.

The dog looks a bit worried; I expect it feels insecure. Roy spent the day asleep on the toolshed roof, unaware of the trouble it was causing.

Saturday July 24th

Went shopping for holiday clothes today. My mother came with me. I wanted to buy a grey zip-up cardigan from Marks and Spencer (there is a cold wind at Skegness). I tried it on but my mother said it made me look like Frank Bough and refused to pay for it. We had a bit of an argument about my taste in clothes versus her taste in clothes. In fact, looking around, I could see quite a few teenagers were having arguments with their parents.

We walked around the rest of the shops without speaking for a bit until my mother dragged me into a punk shop and tried to interest me in a lime-green leopard-skin-print tee-shirt. I refused to try the tasteless thing on, so she bought it for herself!

The sadistic-looking shop assistant said, 'That's a cool mother you got.' I pretended not to hear him. It wasn't difficult: Sid Vicious was singing a filthy version of 'My Way' on the shop's stereo system. It was so loud that the chain jackets and studded belts were reverberating.

Our next stop was at Mothercare, where my mother went mad buying miniature clothes and stretch-mark cream. I was hoping that she would buy a nice respectable maternity dress for the dreaded day when her lump starts to show, but she informed me that she was intending to carry on wearing her dungarees. I will be a laughing-stock at school.

Sunday July 25th
SEVENTH AFTER TRINITY

Did a bit of 'O' level revising. I've got the lousy stinking mocks to do when I get back to school. I am doing English, Geography and History at 'O' level and Woodwork and Domestic Science and Biology at CSE.

It's all a big waste of time, though, because intellectuals like me don't need qualifications to get jobs or worldly success: it just comes automatically to us. It is because of our rarity value. The only problem is getting influential people to *recognize* that you are an intellectual. So far nobody has recognized it in me, yet I have been using long words like 'multi-structured' in my daily intercourse for ages.

Monday   July 26th

Courtney Elliot brought bad news this morning. It was a letter from the Manpower Services Commission telling my father that his canal bank clearance project was 'seriously behind schedule'. My father stormed on and on about, 'What do they expect if they pay slave wages?'

My mother said (quite mildly for her), 'Well you've hardly *worked* like a slave, George. You're always home by four-thirty.'

My father went out and slammed the kitchen door. I ran after him and offered to help him on the canal bank, but he said, 'No, stay at home and help your mother with the holiday packing.'

My mother and Courtney Elliot were doing the *Guardian* crossword together, and the holiday clothes were still in the Ali Baba basket waiting to be washed so I took the dog round to Bert's and watched the Falklands Memorial Service on television.

St Paul's Cathedral was full of widows and bereaved people. I went home and chucked my Falklands campaign map in the bin.

Tuesday   July 27th
MOON'S FIRST QUARTER

My mother had a pompous note from Pandora's father today. He is refusing to give Pandora £120 for Skegness!

The mean git says that he has already forked out four hundred quid for a canoeing holiday down the Wye for his family in September, and Pandora's made-to-measure wet suit was costing forty quid so he was 'unable to stretch his finances further.' So, a fortnight without Pandora looms ahead, unless I can think of a way to make £120 in a hurry. Pandora hasn't got any money of her own; she spends all her pocket money on viola strings.

Wednesday   July 28th

My mother's lump started showing today, but she is doing nothing to disguise it. In fact she seems quite *proud* of it. She is showing it to everybody who comes to the house.

I have to go out of the room.

Thursday   July 29th

My father has been working flat out on the canal bank for the past three days. He hasn't been getting home until 10 p.m. at night. He is getting dead neurotic about leaving it and going on holiday.

Went to see Queenie in hospital. She is on a ward full of old ladies with sunken-in white faces. It's a good job that Queenie was wearing her rouge, I wouldn't have recognized her without it.

Queenie can't speak properly so it was dead embarrassing trying to work out what she was saying. I left after twenty minutes, worn out with smiling. I tried not to look at the old ladies as I walked back down the ward, but it didn't stop them shouting out to me and waving. One of them asked me to fetch a nice piece of cod for her husband's tea. The tired-looking nurse said that a lot of the old ladies were living in the past. I can't say I really blame them; their present is dead horrible.

Friday   July 30th

Our family went to Pandora's house to discuss what was involved in looking after Bert while we are on holiday.

Bert grumbled all the way through the meeting. He's never a bit grateful for anything you do for him. Sometimes I wish he *would* go and live in the Alderman Cooper Sunshine Home.

My mother gave this list to Pandora's mother:

1. He will only drink out of the George V Coronation cup.
2. He takes three heaped spoons of sugar in tea.

3. Don't let him watch *Top of the Pops*; it over-excites him.
4. District Nurse comes on Tuesdays to check for pressure sores.
5. He'll *only* eat beetroot sandwiches, scrambled eggs, Vesta curries and various Dream Toppings. Don't waste your energy in trying to extend his range. I've tried and failed.
6. He moves his bowels at 9.05 a.m. precisely. So please make sure you arrive at his bungalow in plenty of time to arrange the commode.
7. Sabre needs *at least* a four-mile walk *every day*. Any less and he becomes quite impossible.
8. Don't talk to Bert during *Crossroads*.
9. Mrs Singh will cover for you in an emergency, but she *must* be chaperoned.
10. He's OK to be left at night providing he's had his quota of brown ales (THREE BOTTLES).
11. He'll accuse you of fiddling him out of his pension. Ignore him.
12. *The Best of British Luck!*

Saturday   July 31st

Rio Grande Boarding House, Skegness

Pandora came round early this morning to say goodbye; normally I would have been in anguish at the prospect of being without her for two weeks, but I was too busy packing my cases and looking for my swimming trunks to break down. Pandora helped me by packing my medical supplies for me. We finally left our cul-de-sac at 6 p.m.

The car broke down at Grantham so we didn't arrive at the Rio Grande until 12.30. The boarding house was locked and in complete darkness. We stood on the steps ringing the bell for ages, eventually a miserable-looking bloke unlocked the door. He said 'Mole Family? Yer late. These doors are locked at 11 p.m. an' there's a 50p fine for latecomers.'

My mother said, 'And whom might you be?'

The man said, 'I'm Bernard Porke, that's whom I am – Proprietor of the Rio Grande.'

My mother said, 'Well, thank you for your effusive welcome, Mr Porke.' She signed the register while I went and helped my father get the cases off the roof rack.

The tarpaulin had disappeared somewhere *en route*, so everything was wet through. I am writing this in my basement room. It overlooks the dustbins. I can hear Mr and Mrs Porke quarrelling in the kitchen next door.

I wish I was back in the Midlands.

Sunday   August 1st
EIGHTH AFTER TRINITY. LAMMAS (SCOTTISH QUARTER DAY)

I was woken up by Mr Porke shouting, 'Only one piece of bacon per plate, Beryl. Are you trying to ruin me?'

I got dressed quickly and ran up six flights of stairs to my parents' attic room. Woke them up and told them that breakfast was nearly ready. My father told me to run down to the dining room and bag a decent table. (He is experienced in seaside boarding houses.)

I sat at a table next to the massive picture window and watched my fellow boarders take their places at the tables. For some reason everyone was whispering. Mothers kept telling their children to sit still, sit up straight, etc. Fathers stared at the cruet.

My parents' arrival caused a bit of a stir. My mother never keeps her voice down, so everyone heard her complaining about the nylon sheets, including Mr Porke. I'm sure that's why our table only got two pieces of fried bread.

Monday   August 2nd
BANK HOLIDAY (SCOTLAND). HOLIDAY (REPUBLIC OF IRELAND)

My father has gone back to his proletarian roots. He bought a

'Kiss me Quick, Squeeze me Slowly' hat and walked along the promenade swigging out of a can of lager.

I wore my dark glasses and kept well behind him.

Tuesday   August 3rd

Eleven days to go and I have already spent all my money on the slot machines.

Wednesday   August 4th
FULL MOON

The sun came out today!

Also Prince William was christened. The Rio Grande celebrated by giving everyone an extra boiled egg at tea time.

Thursday   August 5th

A man called Ray Peabody has joined our table. He is a divorcee from Corby. He spent his *honeymoon* at the Rio Grande. (No wonder he is divorced.) He comes to Skegness to take part in the talent contests. He is a singer and juggler. He showed us a bit of juggling with the cruet until Mr Porke told him to 'stop abusing the facilities.'

Friday   August 6th

Sent Pandora a donkey postcard.

> Dear Pan,
> The sun came out on Wednesday, but it didn't reach into the black despair caused by our separation. It is a cultural desert here.
> Thank God I have brought my Nevil Shute books.
> Yours unto infinity.
> Adrian X

Saturday   August 7th

Went to Gibraltar Point in the car to see the wild-life sanctuary.

Saw the sanctuary but no wild life. I expect they were all sheltering from the wind.

Read *The Cruel Sea* by a bloke called Nicholas something.

Sunday   August 8th
NINTH AFTER TRINITY

My father went on a sea fishing trip today with the Society of Redundant Electric Storage Heater Salesmen.

My mother and I spent the day on the beach reading the Sunday papers. She is quite nice when you get her on her own. The sun was dead hot but I've got eighteen spots on my shoulders so I couldn't take my shirt off.

Monday   August 9th

We bought day tickets and went to a holiday camp today.

The sight of all the barbed wire and the pale listless people walking aimlessly around inside gave me a weird feeling.

My father started whistling 'The Bridge on the River Kwai' and it *was* like being in a prisoner of war camp. Nobody was actually tortured or starved, but you got the feeling that the attendants could turn quite nasty. My parents went straight to a bar, so I went on all the pathetic free rides, watched a knobbly knees competition, then a tug of war, then I stood outside the bar waiting for my parents.

They had selfishly chosen a 'No under-eighteens' bar.

At 1.30 my father came out with a bottle of Vimto and a packet of crisps for me.

At 2.30 I put my head round the door and asked how long they would be. My father snarled, 'Stop whining. Go and find something to do.' I watched the Donkey Derby for a bit then got fed up and went and sat in the car.

At 4 p.m. a loudspeaker shouted, 'Would Adrian Mole aged fifteen please go to the lost children's centre where his mummy and daddy are waiting for him.'

The humiliation!

The torment of being given a lollipop by a morose attendant!

My parents thought it was dead funny; they laughed all the way back to the ranch.

Tuesday   August 10th

During the evening meal Mr Porke brought my father a message to say that a close friend had been taken into the Royal Hospital and would he please ring ward twelve immediately. It was a mystery to all of us. My father hasn't got any close friends.

My father left the table in a panic. My mother got up to follow him but he said, 'No Pauline, it's got nothing to do with you.'

He was gone for about fifteen minutes, when he came back he said, 'I've got something to tell you both, let's go somewhere private.'

We sat in a wind shelter on the promenade and he informed me and my mother that he was the father of Stick Insect's one-day-old baby boy.

About sixty hours passed, then my mother said, 'What's he called?'

My father said, '*Brett*. Sorry.'

I couldn't think of anything to say so I kept quiet. I still can't think of anything to say so I am going to sleep.

Wednesday   August 11th

12.30 p.m. My father has gone to see Brett and Stick Insect. My mother made him go.

I can't think of anything to say to my mother. I always knew I had no small talk, and now I know I've got no big talk either.

8 p.m. She just sits in her attic room with her hands over her lump. She hasn't cried once, I am dead worried.

9 p.m. I phoned Pandora's mother and told her everything. She was very sympathetic. She said she would get Bert settled for the night and then drive to Skegness and pick us up.

I packed all the suitcases and made my mother wash her face and do her hair, then we sat and waited for Mrs Braithwaite.

Thursday   August 12th
MOON'S LAST QUARTER

Home.

11 p.m. As soon as she saw Mrs Braithwaite my mother started to cry. Mrs Braithwaite said, 'They're *all* bastards, Pauline,' and gave ME a filthy look! It's just not fair! I intend to stay completely and totally true to Pandora. All else is chaos.

We got home at 4.30 a.m. this morning. Mrs Braithwaite doesn't like driving over 30 mph.

I went straight to bed. I didn't dare to check to see if my father was in his room.

Friday   August 13th

The day augured ill.

My father's razor had gone from out of the bathroom so I was forced to use my mother's pink underarm one. It cut my face to ribbons (but there was a very satisfactory amount of bristle around the side of the washbasin).

I had to have a shave because Grandma came round to be told the awful news that her son had fathered an illegitimate child, whilst his wife of fourteen years was expecting a legitimate one.

Grandma took it quite well. She said, 'Which hospital is this woman in?' My mother told her and she straightened her hat and left in a taxi.

Pandora told me that her mother is close to having a nervous breakdown because Bert Baxter has been playing her up all week.

Personally, myself, I think the world has gone mad. Barry Kent won the 'Off the Street' Youth Club poetry competition. His grinning moronic face was in the evening paper. I can't take much more.

Saturday   August 14th

Grandma has gone over to the other side!

She has given some of *our* baby's clothes to Brett Slater, Stick Insect's son. I know Grandma doesn't like my mother, but at least my mother is my father's legal wife.

I am just about sick and tired of adults! They have the nerve to tell kids what to do and then they go ahead and break all their own rules.

Pandora's father came round this morning to ask my mother if she wanted any help. My mother said, 'Bugger off home and help your own wife.' At this rate she'll have no men friends left.

Barclays Bank was open this morning. I bet my father was first in the queue. He always forgets to go on Fridays.

Sunday   August 15th
TENTH AFTER TRINITY

My father came round and asked if he could come home. I wanted my mother to say yes, but she said no. So my father has gone to live with Grandma.

The rat fink has taken the stereo with him. My mother says she doesn't care, she says that after her baby is born she is going to get a highly paid job and buy the best stereo system in the world.

Monday   August 16th

Pandora shocked me today by asking if I was curious about my '*brother Brett*'. It's dead strange to think I've got a brother. I hope the poor kid has better luck with his skin than me.

Tuesday   August 17th

A cheque for fifty pounds arrived today from my father. My mother ripped it up and posted the pieces back. How stupid can you get?

Even my mother regretted it later on.

Stick Insect, Maxwell House and Brett have moved into Grandma's house.

Wednesday   August 18th

Took the dog for a walk and called casually round to
Grandma's and casually looked into Brett Slater's cot. The
kid's skin is covered in white flaky stuff. He's got loads of
wrinkles as well.

I didn't see Stick Insect or my father. Grandma was teaching
Maxwell manners at the tea table.

I didn't stay long. I didn't tell my mother I had been, either. It
was only a casual visit.

Thursday   August 19th
NEW MOON

Mrs Braithwaite is on Librium because of Bert Baxter, so Mrs
Singh has taken over her duties. I haven't seen Bert for ages. I
know he will make crude comments about my father's virility,
so I am keeping away.

I have gone right off sex. It seems to cause nothing but
trouble, especially to women.

Friday   August 20th

My mother is too depressed to do any cooking so I am having to
do it. So far we have had salad with either corned beef or tuna,
but I think I will try something different tomorrow – ham
perhaps.

My father keeps ringing up to see how my mother is. Today
he asked me if she had mentioned divorce. I said no, she hadn't
mentioned it but she certainly looked as if she was thinking
about it.

Saturday   August 21st

Casually called in at Grandma's again. Brett has got my father's
big nose. Grandma was changing his yukky nappy. I was
amazed at how big his thing is.

Stick Insect is *breastfeeding* Brett. (The poor kid must be hungry because the last time I had a close look she hadn't got any breasts.)

My father and Stick Insect were out, buying baby equipment between feeds.

Sunday   August 22nd
ELEVENTH AFTER TRINITY

Went out and bought the Sunday papers, but didn't bother sneaking a look at the *News of the World* behind the greetings card rack like I usually do. I've got enough sex scandals in my own family without reading about anyone else's.

Mr Cherry, the newsagent, asked if he was to cancel my father's fishing and DIY magazines. I told him to go ahead.

The papers weighed 3 lbs, but there was nothing in them apart from the PLO fleeing from Beirut again.

Monday   August 23rd

Barry Kent's mother has had another baby; Pandora passed by the church just as the Kents were emerging from the Christening service. She said the baby looked just like all the other Kents – fierce eyes and massive fists.

They have called the baby Clarke, after Superman. Yuk! Yuk! Yuk!

Tuesday   August 24th

Mrs Singh has arranged for Bert to go on holiday with some charity for elderly Hindus. I asked how long Bert had been a Hindu. Mrs Singh said, 'I don't care if he's not a Hindu. I don't care if he's a Moonie or a Divine Light Missionary so long as he is far away from me.'

Sabre is staying at the RSPCA hostel. I hope he is in isolation for the sake of the other dogs.

Wednesday   August 25th

Courtney Elliot was sipping Brazilian coffee in the kitchen when I came downstairs. He said, 'I bear an important missive for Master Mole.' It was a letter from the BBC!

I took the letter up to my room and stared at it, willing it to say, 'Yes we are giving you an hour-long poetry programme; it will be called "Adrian Mole, a Youth and his Poetry".'

I wanted it to say that, but of course it didn't. It said:

British Broadcasting Corporation
19th July

Dear Adrian Mole,

Thank you for your very neat letter and for the new poem entitled 'Norway'. It is a considerable development on your previous work and indicates that you are maturing as a poet. If your School Magazine rejected 'Norway' then the Editor of the magazine probably needs his (or her) head seeing to. Unless, of course, you have a lot of very good poets at your school. I agree with you about those boring rhyming poems about flowers and stuff but you must remember that before you can break the rules of rhyme and rhythm you do have to know what those rules are about. It is like a painter who wishes to do abstract paintings – he has to know how to draw precisely from life before he jumbles things up. Picasso is a very good case in point to cite.

I hope you were successful in your test on the Norwegian Leather Industry. The Norwegian colleague (he is a Radio Producer in Bergen, Norway) to whom I showed your poem was very impressed that you were studying his country so diligently. I attach a translation of a letter he sent you which must have been rather difficult to understand since it was in Norwegian. Incidentally, I think 'Fjords' is a better word than 'Inlets'. Don't worry about the spelling, a good editor will always correct details like that. I like your use of the explosive 'But!' in the penultimate line. There isn't anything practical I can do with this particular work but I will put it on the file as an *aide memoire* to your progress as a poet (remember there is not much money in poetry ...).

I seldom get to see Terry Wogan in the corridors as he works in Radio Two and I work for Radios Three and Four. Also his show goes on the air very early and he has usually left the building by the time I get to my desk.

With my best wishes and again my thanks for having let me see your latest work.

> Yours sincerely,
> John Tydeman (Radio Four)

Dear Adrian

John Tydeman showed me your poem 'Norway' and I was very moved by its sentiments. I hope you will be able to visit our country one day. It is very beautiful and you will be able to visit the Fjords and see where Ibsen and Grieg lived. As an intellectual, this should be of interest to you. Perhaps when you visit us and speak with us you will not find our vowels so strange. Remember we only have long nights and short days in winter. In June it is the opposite. So come in summer and we will make you very welcome.

Good luck with your study of the Norwegian Leather industry.

> Yours sincerely,
> Knut Johansen

What a brilliant letter! 'Considerable Development', 'Maturing as a Poet'! The translation was even better; it was an invitation to go to Norway! Well, almost. There was no actual mention of paying my fare, but, 'Come in summer, we will make you very welcome'!

My mother and Courtney Elliot read the letters. Courtney said, 'You have a very singular son, Mrs Mole.'

My mother's reply was brief yet touching. 'I know,' she said.

Thursday   August 26th
MOON'S FIRST QUARTER

I tackled Courtney Elliot about the late delivery of my BBC
letter, which was dated July 19th so had taken over a month to
travel 104 miles. Courtney said, 'I believe that there was a
derailment of the Mail Train at Kettering in July. It is possible
that your letter was in one of those unfortunate mail bags that
lay at the bottom of the embankment until being discovered by
a homeward-bound ploughman.'
   The Post Office have always got an excuse!

Friday   August 27th

The bank rate has been reduced to 10½% so my mother has
made an appointment to see Mr Niggard, the Bank Manager.
She wants to borrow some money because she hasn't got any
left.
   I hope she gets a loan; I haven't had any pocket money for
two weeks.

Saturday   August 28th

Pandora is taking canoeing lessons in preparation for her River
Wye holiday. She had her first lesson today and she invited me
to watch and, if necessary, give her the kiss of life in case she fell
out and nearly drowned.
   She looked dead erotic in her black wetsuit and crash
helmet. And for the first time in yonks I felt my thing moving on
its own.
   I can't remember anything more about the lesson, so was
unable to join in Pandora's enthusiastic conversation on the
way home in her dad's car.

Sunday   August 29th
TWELFTH AFTER TRINITY

Stayed in bed all day. My mother went to a picnic with some

women at a place called Greenham Common. It was dark when she got back. I was dead worried.

Monday   August 30th
LATE SUMMER HOLIDAY (UK EXCEPT SCOTLAND)

My mother was happy today. She cleaned the house from top to bottom (including the cutlery drawer and understairs cupboard). She sang the same song over and over again.

> You can't kill the spirit
> She is like a mountain
> Old and strong.
> She goes on and on and on!

It looks like her picnic did her good.

Tuesday.   August 31st

My mother went to see the Bank Manager this morning. I persuaded her to put a loose dress on so that he wouldn't know she was pregnant.

But it turned out that my father had already been whining to the bank for money and while he was there he had blabbed out all our family secrets. Mr Niggard knew that the only income my mother has is Social Security and Family Allowance so he wouldn't lend her any more.

He said she was a bad risk. There is nothing for it, I will have to get a Saturday job. I need money desperately, I've got two months' library fines to pay.

Wednesday   September 1st

Got a card from Bert Baxter. It was a picture of Bradford Town Hall. Bert had written,

> Dear Laddo,
> Having a good laugh with the old 'uns, we are visiting temples and going to weddings nearly every day. The grub is good but I've had to knock off the drink on

account of the other old 'uns' religion.

Queenie is coming out next week. So be a good lad and nip round and give the bungalow a bit of a tidy up.

Yours affec'ly,
Bert

Pandora took her One-Star Canoeing test this afternoon. Her instructor, a bloke called Bill Sampson, said that Pandora has got 'great canoeing potential'. He raved on about Pandora's powerful shoulders, limp wrists and gripping thighs. Pandora passed her test easily. Bill Sampson has offered to prepare her for her Two-Star Test.

Pandora has asked me to join her in her new hobby, but I have got a morbid dread of capsizing so I declined. I am quite happy watching from the bank thinking my intellectual thoughts and holding the towels and thermos flask.

Thursday   September 2nd

There is now no disguising the fact that my mother is pregnant. She sticks right out at the front and walks in a very peculiar manner. She finds it a bit difficult to bend down, so I spend half my time picking things up for her.

Her dungarees are too tight for her, so I am hoping that she will buy a pretty flowery maternity dress. Princess Diana looked charming during her pregnancy. One of those big white collars would really suit my mother. Also it would distract attention from her wrinkly neck.

Friday   September 3rd
FULL MOON

Pandora and her parents are leaving for the River Wye tomorrow. I have offered to go in and feed Marley, their big ginger cat. They have accepted my kind offer and have entrusted me with their keys. It is a massive responsibility, their house is chock-a-block with expensive electrical items and ancient antiques.

Saturday   September 4th

Waved goodbye to my love today. She blew kisses from the rear windows of the Volvo Estate then vanished round the corner.

I waited half an hour (in case they came back for something they had forgotten) then I let myself into the house, made myself a cup of coffee and sat down to watch their big colour telly. At dinner-time I made myself a tuna sandwich (must remember to replace the tin of tuna before they come back) and ate it at Mr Braithwaite's desk.

I couldn't help noticing a letter on his desk:

> Dear Chairperson,
> Arthur, it is with the deepest regret that I offer my resignation as vice-chairperson of the Elm Ward Labour Party.
> The Committee has moved so far to the right recently that I now find my own moderate views are regarded by them as 'extremist'.
> As you know I objected to the Committee sending a telegram of congratulations to Mrs Thatcher during the Falklands Crisis, and, because of my objections, I was called a 'Stalinist' and a 'traitor'. Mrs Benson told me to get back to Russia where I belong.
> I know she is a stalwart party member and is indispensable at collecting the tea money, but her constant talk about the Royal Family has no place at a Labour Party meeting, especially with unemployment as high as it is.
> And finally and sadly, your own comments about Tony Benn I find absolutely repellent. Calling a member of your own party a 'goggle-eyed goon' is just not on, Arthur. Tony Benn has served this country well in the past, and he may well lead it one day.
> I am going on holiday for a week. I will speak to you when I get back.
> Yours,
> Ivan Braithwaite

There was a stamped, addressed envelope lying next to the letter. Mr Braithwaite had obviously been too busy to post it himself so I posted the letter on my way home.

Sunday   September 5th

I have just been to see a brilliant play at our neighbourhood centre. It was called *Woza Albert*. It was all about South Africa and how cruel their government is to the black people who do all the work. I cried a bit at the end. I swear I will never eat another Cape apple as long as I live.

Monday   September 6th
LABOUR DAY (USA AND CANADA)

Spent all day watering the Braithwaites' plants. It can't be healthy living amongst so much vegetation. It's a wonder Pandora and her parents don't die of oxygen starvation. If I was them I would keep a caged canary around the place.

Tuesday   September 7th

Went to the ante-natal clinic with my mother. We waited for two hours in a room full of red-faced pregnant women. My mother had forgotten to bring a sample of urine from home, so a nurse gave her a shiny oven tray and told her to, 'Squeeze a few drops out for us, dear.'

My mother had only just been to the loo so she took ages and ended up missing her place in the weighing queue. By the time her blood pressure was taken my mother was in a state of hypertension. She said the doctor warned her about doing too much and told her to relax more.

Wednesday   September 8th

Realized with horror that school starts next Monday and I have only done one day's revising for my mock exams. Took my History folder round to the Braithwaites', fed the cat and settled down in the study. I thought perhaps the studious atmosphere might help but I can't say it made much difference. I still can't remember Archduke Ferdinand's middle name, or the date of the Battle of Mons.

Thursday   September 9th

Went round to Bert Baxter's bungalow to tidy up. Queenie is coming home from hospital on Saturday. I hope the Hindus bring Bert back in time.

Did revision for mocks until 3 a.m.

Friday   September 10th
MOON'S LAST QUARTER

Courtney Elliot said, 'A billet-doux for the Young Master.' It was a letter from Pan.

Adrian Precious,
We started at Builth Wells on Sunday evening and had quite an exciting paddle downstream. Mummy and Daddy were paddling an open Canadian. I was in a single kayak.

We camped overnight at Llanstephan. It was lovely, I left the flap of my tent open and looked up at the stars and thought of you.

Just beyond Llanstephan there is an orgiastic rapid called Hell Hole. The local people fear it and all the canoeing guides describe it as being 'Grade Three, must be portaged', which means you mustn't canoe down it, but instead carry your canoe and equipment *around* it.

Mummy and Daddy managed to get to the side of the river OK but the water carried me ever onwards towards Hell Hole. Honestly Adrian, it was just like *Deliverance*, I half expected a Welsh halfwit to appear on the bridge and start twanging a harp.

Anyway I went rushing into Hell Hole and the canoe turned upside down, but I managed to get out after a

while. My boat was smashed in half, but I regained
consciousness and swam to the bank.

    See you on Sunday.
        All my love,
        Pandora

P.S. Mummy's nerves are off again.

I felt ill after reading Pandora's letter. I had to take a junior
aspirin and lie down.

Saturday   September 11th

Had horrible nightmares all night. I kept seeing Pandora's body
floating under the remains of Skegness Pier.

Sunday   September 12th
FOURTEENTH AFTER TRINITY

Everybody returned home today apart from my father.

    Ironed my school uniform: it is much too small for me, but
my mother can't afford a new one.

Monday   September 13th

I am now a fifth-year and have the privilege of using the side
entrance of the school. I can't wait until next year when I will be
able to use the *front* entrance (sixth formers and staff only).

    Perhaps I have got a perverted streak, but I really enjoyed
watching the first-, second-, third- and fourth-years cramming
through their low status entrance at the back of the school.

    I informed Mrs Claricoates, the school secretary that once
again I am on free school dinners. As usual she was full of
empathy for me and said, 'Never mind, pet, it'll all come out in
the wash.'

    Had mock English exam. I was the first to finish. It was a
doddle.

Tuesday   September 14th

I have got a new form teacher. His name is Mr Lambert. He is the kind of teacher who likes being friendly. He said, 'Consider me a friend, any problems to do with school or home, I want to hear them.'

He sounded more like a Samaritan than a teacher. I have made an appointment to see him after school tomorrow.

My mother is thirty-eight today. I bought her a card which said 'Happy 18th Birthday', *but*, I cunningly changed the number one into a three by the use of Tipp-Ex and dried lentils. So it read 'Happy 38th Birthday!' Unfortunately the verse on the inside didn't match my mother's lifestyle much.

> A-tremble on the edge of life,
> One day to be a mum and wife.
> But now it's discos fun and laughter:
> Why should you care what's coming after?

The picture on the front was of a teenage girl going mad to sounds coming out of a record player. On reflection, I think it was a bad choice of card. I wish I wasn't an impulse buyer. Her present was some underarm hair remover. I noticed that the stuff she usually uses had run out.

My father sent a card picturing a sad cat. He had written inside 'Yours as ever, George.' That stinking rat Lucas sent a card from Sheffield. It was in a box and had a cartoon mouse on the front eating a piece of cheese (Edam I think). Inside Lucas had written: 'Pauline, I'll never forget that night in the pinewoods. Yours with undying love, Bimbo.'

She had ten other cards, all from women and all with pictures of flowers on the front. I don't know why women are so mad about flowers. Personally they leave me cold. I prefer trees.

Wednesday   September 15th

My father phoned up before I went to school this morning. He wanted to speak to my mother, but she refused to talk to him.

Brett was crying. In the background, it sounded as if Grandma and Stick Insect were quarrelling. Somebody (it could only have been Maxwell I suppose) was playing a toy xylophone. My father sounded dead miserable. He said, 'I know I did wrong, Adrian; but the punishment hardly fits the crime.'

Had a long talk with Mr Lambert after school. He took me to a café and bought me a cup of tea and a vanilla slice. As we parted he said, 'Look, Adrian, try to detach yourself from the mess your parents are in. You're a *gifted boy* and you mustn't let them drag you down to their level.'

'*A gifted boy*'! At last someone apart from Pandora has recognized my intellectual prowess.

Had mock biology exam. I was the last to finish.

Thursday   September 16th

Barry Kent has made an appointment with Mr Lambert to talk about *his* family problems!

I hope Mr Lambert has got twenty-four hours to spare. Ha! Ha! Ha!

Had mock geography exam. Just my luck – there were no questions about the Norwegian Leather Industry.

Friday   September 17th
NEW MOON

Nearly everyone in our class has made an appointment to see Mr Lambert about their family problems. Even Pandora, whose mother is a Marriage Guidance Counsellor!

Mr Lambert is going about the school biting his nails and looking worried. He has stopped taking people to the café.

Saturday   September 18th

A Tydeman letter! Alas, yet another rejection. The gods are not yet smiling on me.

British Broadcasting Corporation
17th September

Dear Adrian Mole

Thank you for your latest letter (undated – you must, if you are going to be a writer – and even if you are not – DATE your letters. We file them, you know. The BBC has lots of files, some of which are kept in warehouses in Ware, Herts, others of which are at Caversham, nr Reading. Some of the files are very valuable.)

The country seems to have made you gloomy. It often makes poets gloomy, people like Wordsworth & Co. On other occasions it uplifts them – skylarks singing, lambs bounding, daffodils daffing, waterfalls crashing. It provokes odes and things in them. So forget gloom and suicide and write something cheerful.

I'm afraid that the poem is not yet up to broadcast standard but it does show a poetic advance, so keep on trying. We will naturally respect your copyright in your work. (The BBC is usually very good about things like that.) Copyright is dealt with by a special department and we do not bother the Director General directly with such matters. However, you have not got your break (chance) – yet.

Do not kill yourself because of another rejection. If all poets killed themselves because of early rejections there would be no poetry at all.

Yours most sincerely,
John Tydeman

Sunday   September 19th
FIFTEENTH AFTER TRINITY

Took a deep breath and went to see Bert and Queenie today. They were hostile to me because I've neglected them for a week.

Bert said, 'He's not bothered about us old 'uns no more, Queenie. He's more interested in gadding about.'

How unfair can you get? I can't remember the last time I gadded about. Queenie didn't say anything because she can't speak properly because of the stroke, but she certainly *looked* antagonistic.

Bert ordered me to come back tomorrow to clean up. Their home help comes on Tuesdays and Bert likes the place to be tidy for when she comes.

Monday   September 20th

Courtney Elliot didn't bring my mother's Social Security giro this morning. I went to school worrying about it and hoping it would come in the second post. I was amazed to learn that I'd only got average marks for my mocks. Surely there has been a serious error.

Tuesday   September 21st

My mother and Courtney Elliot had a row over the missing giro this morning. Courtney said, 'Don't shoot the messenger because the news is bad or non-existent, Mrs Mole.'

My mother tried to ring the Social Security Office all day, but the line was permanently engaged.

Wednesday   September 22nd

I skived off school and went to the Social Security offices with my mother. She couldn't face going on her own. I'm certainly glad I went because it was no place for a pregnant woman.

My mother joined the queue of complaining people at the reception desk. And I sat down on the screwed-down chairs.

The reception clerk was hiding behind a glass screen, so everyone was forced to shout out their most intimate financial secrets to her. I heard my mother shouting with the rest, then she came back holding a ticket numbered 89, and said that we would have to wait until our number was displayed on an electronic screen.

We waited for yonks amongst what my mother called 'The

casualties of Society'. (My father would have described them as 'dregs'.) A group of tramps staggered about singing and arguing with each other. Toddlers ran amok. Teenage mothers shouted and smacked. A Teddy boy on crutches lurched up the stairs helped by an old skinhead in ragged Doc Martens. Everyone ignored the 'No Smoking' notices and stubbed their cigarettes out on the lino. The respectable people stared down at their shoes. About every ten minutes a number flashed up on the screen and somebody got up and went through a door marked 'Private Interviews'.

I didn't see any of the people who'd gone through the door *come out* again. I thought this was a bit sinister. My mother said, 'They've probably got gas chambers out there.'

Our private interview was against the Trades Description Act, because it wasn't private at all. The interviewer was also behind a glass screen, so my mother had to bellow out that she hadn't received her giro and was financially destitute.

The interviewer said, 'Your giro was posted on Friday, Mrs Moulds.'

'MRS MOULDS?' said my mother, 'My name's Mole – MOLE – as in furry mammal.'

'Sorry,' said the interviewer, 'I've got the wrong records.'

We waited another fifteen minutes, then he came back and said, 'Your giro will be put in the post tonight.'

'But I need the money now,' my mother pleaded. 'There's no food in the house and my son needs school trousers.'

'There's nothing I can do,' the bloke said wearily. 'Can't you borrow some money?'

My mother looked the man straight in the eyes and said, 'OK will *you* lend me five pounds, please?'

The man said, 'It's against the rules.'

Now I know why the furniture is screwed down. I felt like flinging a chair about myself.

Thursday   September 23rd
AUTUMNAL EQUINOX

No giro. Courtney Elliot lent my mother £5.

Friday   September 24th

8.30 a.m. No giro. But a cheque from my father arrived so we are saved! My mother gave me 15p for a Mars bar, my first in days.

4.30 p.m. My mother took the cheque to the bank this morning, but they wouldn't cash it because it needed four days to clear. Mr Niggard the manager was out officiating at a liquidation, so my mother waited for him to come back then grovelled for a temporary overdraft. Mr Niggard let her have £25.

All this trouble has made my mother's ankles swell up. Somebody is going to pay for this!

Saturday   September 25th
MOON'S FIRST QUARTER

No giro!
Looked Swollen Ankles up in the *Good Housekeeping Family Health Encyclopaedia*. It calls itself the 'Complete Modern Medical Reference Book for the Home', but the index didn't have 'Swollen Ankles'. I used my initiative and looked up 'Pregnancy'. I was interested to see that 'Pregnancy' was adjacent to 'Sex and Reproduction'.
I started reading a section called 'Testes and Sperm' and was astonished to discover that my personal testes make several hundred million sperm *a day*. A DAY! Where do they all go? I know some leak out in the night and some I help to leak occasionally, but what happens to the countless billions that are left swarming around, and what about chaste people like priests? During a lifetime they must collect a trillion trillion. It makes the mind boggle, not to mention the testes.

Sunday   September 26th
SIXTEENTH AFTER TRINITY

Read the whole of 'Sex and Reproduction' in bed last night. Woke up to find a few hundred million sperm had leaked out.

Still, it will give the remaining sperm room to wag their tails about a bit.

Monday   September 27th

No giro!

By a massive stroke of luck we did the storage of semen in human biology today. I was able to give a full and frank account of the life cycle of a sperm.

Mr Southgate the biology teacher was dead impressed. After the lesson he said, 'Mole, I don't know if you've got a natural aptitude for biology or a rather obsessive interest in things sexual. If the former I suggest you change from CSE to 'O' level, if the latter perhaps a chat with the school psychology service may be of use.'

I assured Mr Southgate that my interest was purely scientific.

Tuesday   September 28th

No giro!

Pandora and I went for a walk in the woods after school only to find that a building firm had started to build executive houses in the clearings. Pandora said that the woodlands of England were being sacrificed for saunas, double garages and patio doors.

Some lucky executive is going to have the best conker tree in the Midlands in his back garden. He'll also be as sick as a dog because he'll have Barry Kent's gang chucking sticks at it every autumn. Ha! Ha! Ha!

Went back to Pandora's and watched the Labour Party Conference vote for unilateral disarmament. Mr Braithwaite explained that this means if elected the Labour Party would chuck all their nuclear weapons away. Mrs Braithwaite said, 'Yes and leave us at the mercy of the Soviet threat.' Mr Braithwaite and Mrs Braithwaite started arguing about multilateral versus unilateral disarmament. The argument got a bit nasty and Mr Braithwaite went on to accuse his wife of posting a letter of resignation to the Elm Ward Labour Party. Mrs Braithwaite shouted, 'For the last time, Ivan, I did not post that sodding letter.'

Pandora walked me home and explained that since her mother had joined the SDP her parents had worked in separate studies. She said, 'They are intellectually incompatible.'

I asked Pandora about the letter of resignation. She said that her father had written a letter but decided not to post it. He was therefore hurt when his resignation had been accepted. Pandora said, 'Poor Daddy is in the political wilderness.'

Wednesday   September 29th
MICHAELMAS DAY (QUARTER DAY)

No giro!

My mother had a letter from the bank to tell her that my father's cheque had bounced. I was sent round to Grandma's on my way to school to break the news.

Stick Insect was feeding Brett so I didn't know where to put my eyes. Is it good or bad manners to ignore a suckling baby? I kept my eyes on her neck to be on the safe side.

My grandma was getting Maxwell ready for play school. The poor kid was wrapped in so many layers of clothes that he looked a bit like Scott at the South Pole. Grandma said, 'There's a nip in the air and Maxwell has got a chest.'

My father had gone to the canal bank early, so I left a message with Grandma. She pulled her lips in a straight line and said, 'Another bouncing cheque? Your father ought to take up trampolining.'

I asked Grandma if she ever got fed up with Brett, Maxwell and Stick Insect. Grandma said she thrived on hard work, and it's true, she looks better than when all she had to do was listen to Radio Four all day. She doesn't even listen to 'The World at One' now. Brett doesn't like Robin Day's voice for some reason. It makes him scream and bring his milk up.

Thursday   September 30th

No giro!

Wrote a poem today.

> *Waiting for the Giro*
> The pantry door creaks showing empty Fablon shelves.
> The freezer echoes with mournful electrical whirrings.
> The boy goes ragged trousered to school.
> The woman waits at the letterbox.
> The bills line up behind the clock.
> The dog whimpers empty-bellied in sleep.
> The building society writes letters penned in vitriol.
> The house waits, waits, waits,
> Waits for the giro.

I am reading Philip Larkin's *The Whitsun Weddings*.

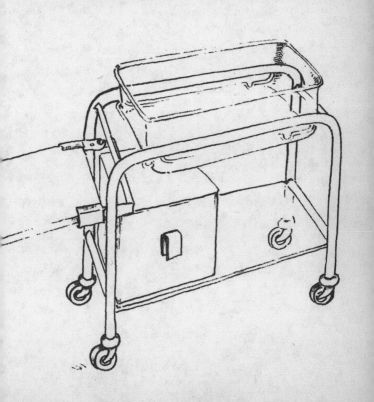

Friday   October 1st

My mother rang up the Citizens' Advice Bureau to find out who her MP is. Then she rang the MP at home, but he wasn't there. His wife said that he had gone on a fact-finding mission to the Canary Isles. She sounded very bitter.

Saturday   October 2nd

Courtney brought a letter from the Fens.

> King Edward Cottage,
> Yosserdyke,
> Norfolk.

Dear Pauline,
Your dad and me was sorry to hear about your trouble and we hopes as it is now cleared up. We never did take to George; he had a hasty temper and we think as how you're better off without him. As regards the money, Pauline, well we only got a few good days at the potato picking so we are a bit short ourselves at the moment, but we enclose a postal order for Adrian, as we know he has got a sweet tooth.

If you would put your trust in the Lord, Pauline, you wouldn't keep having such trouble in your life. God only punishes the heathens and the unbelievers. We was shocked last Christmas as to how much smoking and drinking went on under your roof. You wasn't brought up to it, Pauline. Your dad has never touched a drop in his life, nor has he been a slave to nicotine. We are decent God-fearing folk what knows our place and we only wish that you would take after us more before it's too late.

Uncle Dennis, Auntie Marcia and Cousin Maurice have moved out of the caravan and into a council house. They have got all modern facilities, Auntie Marcia jokes that it is just like Buckingham Palace. Perhaps when you have had the unwelcome baby you will come and see it for yourself.

Anyway Pauline
We are praying for you,
        Yours affectionately,
        Mam and Dad
P.S. Auntie Marcia asks if you ever found Maurice's grey sock that disappeared last Christmas. She's not been able to rest through wondering about it.

Sunday   October 3rd
SEVENTEENTH AFTER TRINITY. FULL MOON

My mother wrote the following reply today:

Dear Mam and Dad,
Sorry about the short delay in replying to your wonderfully comforting letter, but I have only just emerged from a drunken stupor. Adrian was ecstatic to be sent the postal order for 50 pence and rushed straight out to buy me a can of lager. He's such a thoughtful kid.

Nothing would give me greater pleasure than to come down and inspect Auntie Marcia's council house, but I fear that I will be quite unable to drag myself away from the endless round of parties that my life now revolves around. You know what us hedonists are like – living for kicks and not going to church.

I fear that a meticulous search has failed to turn up the missing grey sock. I can appreciate Auntie Marcia's anxiety on this point, so I enclose my last pound note to enable Auntie Marcia to buy a pair and therefore rest in peace.

What you say about George is quite true, but I married him because at that time he laughed a lot. There weren't a lot of laughs in our cottage in the middle of the potato field were there?
        Cordial greetings,
        Your Daughter Pauline
        And Grandson Adrian

I begged her not to send it. She said she would think about it and put it behind the bread bin.

Monday   October 4th

NO GIRO!

Tuesday   October 5th

No giro!

My mother cracked today. She phoned up the local radio station and told them that she was going to abandon her child at the Social Security office unless she was given her giro.

My digital clock radio woke me up to the sound of my own mother's voice telling the airwaves about our financial difficulties. She was downstairs on the hall phone talking to Mitchell Malone, the halfwit DJ. My mother said she was going to abandon me at the Social Security offices unless the SS Manager contacted her by noon.

Mitchell Malone got dead excited and said, 'Listeners, we're in a High Noon situation here. Will Pauline Mole, pregnant single parent, abandon her only child in the Social Security office? Or will Mr Gudgeon, the Social Security office manager who was on this programme last week, present Pauline with her long overdue cheque? Keep tuned for regular updates on Central, your local Radio Station.'

We sat and waited for the phone to ring. At 12.30 my mother said, 'Put your coat on, Adrian, I'm taking you to be abandoned.'

At 12.35 as we were going out of the door the phone rang. It was my father pleading for his name not to be mentioned on the air.

The presence of radio reporters and journalists caused a mini-riot in the Social Security office. All the claimants wanted to tell their stories. The tramps got over-excited and started brawling amongst themselves. The staff staged a walk-out and the police were called.

Mitchell Malone was doing an outside broadcast, he played a record called 'The Lunatics are taking over the Asylum.'

I was only abandoned for forty-five minutes before Mr Gudgeon gave my mother an 'Emergency Needs Payment' of £25. He said it would see us through the weekend. He asked my mother to come in and see him on Monday morning, but a police sergeant said, 'No, Mr Gudgeon, you will go and see Mrs Mole at home.'

Mr Gudgeon sucked his ragged moustache and said, 'But I've got a meeting on Monday morning.'

The sergeant swung his truncheon about and said, 'Yes, your meeting is with Mrs Mole.' Then he strolled off and started knocking the tramps about.

Wednesday   October 6th

A picture of my mother and me was on the front of the paper tonight. (My spots hardly showed up at all.) The headline said: 'A MOTHER'S ANGUISH.' The article underneath said:

> Attractive mother-to-be Pauline Vole (58) took the desperate action of abandoning her only child Adrian (5) in the Carey Street Social Security office yesterday.
>
> Mrs Vole claims to have waited three weeks for a giro cheque. She said, 'I was desperate. Adrian means more to me than life itself, but I was driven to take the drastic step of abandoning him to draw attention to our plight.'
>
> Mr Gudgeon (42) the manager of the Carey Street office, said today: 'Mrs Vole has been the unfortunate victim of a staff shortage. The member of staff who deals with the computer broke his toe drinking squash.'

Thursday   October 7th

The following corrections appeared in the local paper tonight:

> Mrs Pauline Vole would like to correct an inaccurate statement attributed to her in yesterday's edition of the paper.

She did not say, 'Adrian means more to me than life itself.'

In the same article 'drinking squash' should have read 'playing squash'.

We apologize to Mrs Vole and Mr Reginald Gudgeon and thank them for pointing out these unintentional errors.

Friday   October 8th

My mother phoned the local paper to demand that they print the following statement:

Mrs Pauline Mole is 38 and not 58, as was reported in Wednesday's edition.

My mother is fed up with the neighbours talking. Last night Mr O'Leary called out, 'Sure you're a fine-looking woman for your age Mrs Mole.'

Saturday   October 9th
MOON'S LAST QUARTER

The Guinness Book of Records rang up today. A posh bloke spoke to my mother and asked if she would mind her name being included in the 'Oldest Women to Give Birth' section.

He asked my mother to send her birth certificate. My mother said she hadn't given birth yet and she was only thirty-eight.

The bloke said, 'Sorry for troubling you, Mrs Vole,' and rang off.

Read the paper from cover to cover, but nothing about my mother's age appeared tonight.

Sunday   October 10th
EIGHTEENTH AFTER TRINITY

My mother spent the day reading *The Observer* with her ankles raised above her head.

I took the dog out. We went to the woods to see the half-built executive houses.

We explored a house called the 'Winchester'. The dog cocked its leg in the master bedroom and started to squat down on the Bar-B-Q patio so I dragged it away.

Monday   October 11th

Courtney brought a dead exciting postcard. It said:

> Dear Adrian Mole,
> Your work interests me enormously. If you would like to see it published please write to me and I will furnish you with details.
>   Sincerely yours,
>   L. S. Caton

It was sent from an address in Bolton. I wonder how L. S. Caton heard about me? Perhaps Mr Tydeman mentioned me over the dinner table at a BBC banquet.

I sent Mr Caton a short but dignified reply asking for further details.

Gudgeon turned up and gave my mother the rest of her money. On his way out he asked who the men's size ten shoes under the sofa belonged to. My mother told him that they belonged to her son Adrian. She said, 'I'm not likely to start co-habiting in my condition am I?' Mr Gudgeon blushed and tripped over the dog in his haste to get out.

We had a brillo dinner tonight; chicken curry and my mother put a strand of saffron in the rice. We ate it off our knees (to be strictly accurate my mother ate it off her lump) in front of the television while we watched an old Tudor wreck called the *Mary Rose* get dragged up from the sea bottom.

My mother said, 'From what I can see of it the sea bottom is the best place for it.' I was disappointed not to see any skeletons but the commentator told us that it was an historic occasion, so I tried to feel a bit overawed.

Tuesday October 12th

A first-year called Anne Louise Wirgfield asked me for my autograph today. She said, 'I saw your picture in the paper and told my mummy that you go to our school, but mummy said you didn't because the paper said you're only five. So I want your autograph to prove that I know you.'

I gave the kid my autograph, I will have to get used to being pestered one day, I suppose.

Practised my signature all through Maths. Came home; watched the Falklands Task Force marching through London. Looked for Clive Kent, but didn't see him.

Wednesday October 13th

My mother has received a clothing voucher for school trousers from the Social Security. It is made out for £10.

To get the trousers though I have to take the voucher to one of three special shops approved by Social Security. All the shops named – Henry Blogetts and Sons, School Outfitters, Swingin' Sixty's and Mick n' Dave's – are notorious for selling crap clothes at big prices.

I will not demean myself by taking the voucher in. I have put it in my wallet. When I am rich and famous I will look at it and perhaps show it to my friends to prove that I once knew the sour taste of poverty.

Thursday October 14th

Went to see how Brett is getting on today. He seemed to know I was his brother because when I looked into his cot he gave me a daft gummy smile and held on to my finger dead tight.

His skin has cleared up now so perhaps there is hope for the kid.

Grandma is looking dead haggard, but not as haggard as Stick Insect. The two women are getting on each other's nerves. Grandma doesn't approve of Stick Insect using plain flour for Yorkshire puddings and Stick Insect doesn't like the

way Grandma wraps Maxwell's chest up in Vick and brown paper at night. She says the rustling prevents her from sleeping.

When I got home my mother cross-questioned me about Stick Insect and Grandma. She wanted me to recall every expression of face and nuance of voice during my visit.

Friday   October 15th

I have put my name down for the school play. We are doing *The Importance of Being Earnest* by Oscar Wilde.

I am having my audition next Monday. I hope to get to play Ernest, although my mother says the handbag is the best part. She thinks she's such a wit.

Monday   October 18th

The weekend was far, far, far too boring to write about. Mr Golightly, the Drama teacher, stopped me halfway through my *Henry V* speech. He said, 'Look, Adrian, *The Importance of Being Earnest* is a brittle comedy of manners, not a macho war epic. I want to know if you can time a comic line.' He gave me a speech about Victoria Station to read, listened, then said: 'Yes, you'll do.'

I have decided to be an actor when I grow up. I will write my novels during breaks in rehearsal.

Tuesday   October 19th

Mrs Singh accompanied my mother to the ante-natal clinic today. The gynaecologist has told my mother she must rest more or she will be forced into hospital and made to stay in bed. Her swollen ankles are caused by high blood pressure. She is dead old to be having a baby so the doctors are giving her more attention in case she dies and they get into trouble.

Wednesday   October 20th

When I said 'Hello' to Pandora in Geography my voice

wobbled out of control. I kept quiet for the rest of the lesson.

Thursday   October 21st

My mother asked why I was so quiet. She said, 'You've hardly said a word since *Blue Peter*. Is anything wrong?' I shrilled, 'No,' and left the room.

Friday   October 22nd

My voice can't be trusted. One minute it's booming and loud like Ian Paisley, the next it's shrill and shrieking like Margaret Thatcher's used to be before she had voice lessons from an advertising agency.

Saturday   October 23rd

Bert Baxter rang up to tell me that my father has got the sack from Manpower Services. I kept silent. Bert said, 'Ain't you got nought to say?'

I wobbled 'No' and put the phone down. I will have to go to the doctor's about my voice. It can't be normal to suffer like this.

Sunday   October 24th
TWENTIETH AFTER TRINITY
BRITISH SUMMER TIME ENDS

The dog went beserk and ripped the Sunday papers up today. It had no explanation for its bizarre behaviour.

The hall was covered with pieces of newsprint saying 'Ken Livingstone today defended' ... 'Falklands' upkeep rockets to £700 million' ... 'Israeli soldiers watched helpless as' ... 'trouser zips enquiry' ... 'Firemen will accept 7½% but mood is explosive' ...

I swept the pieces up and put them in the dustbin and put the lid on the outside world.

Monday   October 25th
HOLIDAY (REPUBLIC OF IRELAND)
MOON'S FIRST QUARTER

After a silent day at school I took my unstable voice to Dr Gray's surgery. Dr Gray didn't look up from his horrible scribbling, he just said, 'Yes?' I wobbled and shrilled and boomed all my fears about having a defective voice box.

Dr Gray said, 'For Christ's sake it's only your voice breaking, youth! It's come a bit late but then you're physically immature generally. You should take up a physical sport and get more fresh air.'

I asked how long the uncertainty would last.

He said, 'Who knows? I'm not a bloody prophet, am I?'

I could hardly believe my ears. The first thing I do after leaving school will be to take out a subscription to BUPA.

I have resigned from *The Importance of Being Earnest*. To act you need a reliable voice and I haven't got one.

Tuesday   October 26th

Barry Kent has committed educational suicide by wearing his Hell's Angels clothes to school. Mr Lambert pretended not to notice (Barry Kent is four inches taller than him) but Mr Scruton spotted Kent in school dinners and ordered him to take them off, saying that the studs could cause 'somebody to lose an eye.'

Kent went into the fourth-years' cloakroom and took his jacket off. He was wearing a studded death's head shirt underneath so Scruton made him remove that as well, only to reveal a leather-studded vest.

I don't know how Kent manages to carry around so much weight. Mr Scruton has sent Kent home with a note.

Wednesday   October 27th

Some of the more impressionable fourth-years came to school with studs on the back of their blazers.

Thursday   October 28th

Mr Scruton has added another school rule to the million others. Studs are not allowed to be worn anywhere in school except on the soles of sports boots.

After school Pandora and some of her gang rushed out to buy studs to put on the hem of their underskirts.

Friday   October 29th

My mother has the baby in two weeks' time! The hospital did a test on her today. She is getting into a panic because the spare room is still a spare room and not a nursery. We are still dead short of money. The maternity grant only bought half a second-hand pram!

Saturday   October 30th

The dog went berserk again and ripped up my priceless collection of old *Beanos*. I have been collecting them since I was seven so I was heartbroken to see them defiled.

I felt like booting the dog around my bedroom but I let it off lightly by chucking it down the stairs.

It's always respected literature in the past. It will have to go to the vet's, just in case it's got a brain malfunction.

Sunday   October 31st
TWENTY-FIRST AFTER TRINITY. HALLOWE'EN.
DAYLIGHT SAVING TIME ENDS (USA AND CANADA)

At five o'clock I was asked by my so-called best friend Nigel to go to his Hallowe'en party.

He said, 'Forgot to send you an invite, zit face, but come anyway, dress as a warlock or you won't get in.'

I decided not to go as a warlock; I wanted to break away from stereotypes, so I went as a fiend. My mother helped me to assemble a costume. We used my father's old flippers, one of my mother's long-legged black leotards and an orange fright

wig she bought years ago when she went to my father's fishing club dinner and dance.

I looked a bit indecent in the leotard so I put my swimming trunks over the top, but when I got the whole lot on I didn't look a bit fiendish, I just looked dead stupid. My mother had the idea of putting a nylon stocking over my fiendishly made-up face. It looked a bit better but my costume still lacked a certain something.

At seven o'clock I had a crisis of confidence and almost took everything off, but my mother fetched a can of green neon spray paint that we used to perk up last year's Christmas tree. She sprayed me from head to toe with it. The dog whimpered and ran under the draining board. So I knew I must have achieved the right effect.

The short walk to Nigel's house was an ordeal. A gang of little kids in pointed hats ran up to me screaming: 'Trick or Treat.' I kept telling them to bugger off but they followed me to Nigel's, trying to tread on my flippers. Nigel wouldn't let me in at first because I wasn't in warlock costume. (He's so literal! He'll end up working with computers if he's not careful.) But I explained that I was a fiend and he relented. Nigel's mother and father were upstairs watching telly, so we raided their drinks cupboard and drank Tia Maria and Egg Flip Cocktails.

There were no girls at the party, which was a bit strange. Nigel said that girls make him sick. The warlocks and me danced in the pumpkin light to Duran Duran records. It was OK, I suppose, but without girls it lacked a certain *je ne sais quoi* (French for something or other). At ten o'clock Nigel's mother ran in with a running buffet. The food was all gone in ten minutes. Most of it was eaten, but a lot got thrown about. Without the civilizing influence of girls, boys return to the wild.

The school are making me read *Lord of the Flies* by William Golding. I am sharing a book with three dumbos who take half an hour to read one page, so it is turning out to be a frustrating experience.

Monday   November 1st
FULL MOON

After school I went to the hairdresser's with my massive mother. She didn't want me to go but she can't be allowed out of doors on her own, can she? Women are always having babies in phone boxes, buses, lifts etc. It is a well-known fact.

Franco's is run by an Italian bloke. He shouted at my mother as soon as she got through the bamboo door. He said, 'Hey, Pauline, why you no come to see Franco once a week like before, heh?'

My mother explained that she couldn't afford to have her hair done regularly now.

Franco said, 'What foolish thing you say! Hair first, food second. You want your bambino to open his eyes and see an ugly mama?'

I was astonished to hear the way he bossed my mother about, but for once she didn't seem to mind. He wrapped a sheet around her neck and said, 'Sit down, shut up, and keep still,' then he tipped her backwards and shampooed her hair. He told her off for having a few grey hairs and moaned about split ends and the condition. Then he dried her hair in a towel and made her sit in front of a mirror.

My mother said, 'I'll just have a trim please, Franco.'

But Franco said, 'No way, Pauline. I cut it all off and we start again.' And my mother sat there and let him do it!

She also let him spray her bristle-cut hair purple and she paid him for doing it. *And* gave him a tip!

Tuesday   November 2nd

There is a new channel on television. It is called Channel Four and it is for minorities, like intellectuals and people that belong to jigsaw clubs.

At last I have found my spiritual viewing home.

I predict that Channel Four will transform British society. All the morons in the country will start watching it, and get a

taste for education and culture! Yes, Britain is in for a new renaissance!

Wednesday   November 3rd

My mother has packed her little weekend case and put it in the hall.

Thursday   November 4th

My father rang today and asked me how my mother was. I said she was as well as could be expected, for an eight-and-a-half-months pregnant woman.

He asked if the baby's head was engaged yet. I answered coldly that I wasn't conversant with the technicalities of childbirth.

I asked him how his own baby was, he said, 'That's right, Adrian, turn the knife.' Then he put the phone down.

Friday   November 5th
BONFIRE NIGHT!

Locked the dog in the coal shed, as advised by the media. Then went to the Marriage Guidance Council Bonfire party.

It was crowded with couples bickering over the fireworks, so Pandora and I slipped away and shared a packet of sparklers behind the wall of the Co-op bakery. I wrote 'PANDORA' in the air with my sparkler. Pandora wrote 'ADRAIN'. I was very upset: we've been going out for over a year. She ought to know how to spell my name by now.

Went back to the community bonfire and found our dog watching the firework display and chewing a hot-dog.

I lost count of the times nosy adults said, 'That dog should be locked up out of harm's way.'

I tried to explain that our dog is an individualist and can't be treated like other dogs, but what with the exploding of fireworks and the crowds going, 'Oooh!' and, 'Aaaah!' every time a pathetic rocket was launched, it was a bit difficult.

In the end I took the stupid dog home, thus missing the 'Best Dressed Guy' competition.

Saturday   November 6th

Wrote a political poem. I am going to send it to the *New Statesman*. Mr Braithwaite told me that they print a seditious poem every week.

> *Mrs Thatcher by A. Mole*
> Do you weep, Mrs Thatcher, do you weep?
> Do you wake, Mrs Thatcher, in your sleep?
> Do you weep like a sad willow?
> On your Marks and Spencer's pillow?
> Are your tears molten steel?
> Do you weep?
> Do you wake with '*Three million*' on your brain?
> Are you sorry that they'll never work again?
> When you're dressing in your blue, do you see the
> waiting queue?
> Do you weep, Mrs Thatcher, do you weep?

I think my poem is extremely brilliant. It is the sort of poem that could bring the government to its knees.

Sunday   November 7th

Went to see Bert and Queenie with my mother.

Everyone we met on the way asked my mother when the baby was due, or made comments like, 'I expect you'll be glad when the baby's here, won't you?'

My mother was very ungracious in her replies.

Bert opened the door, he said, 'Ain't you dropped that sprog yet?'

My mother said, 'Shut your mouth, you clapped-out geriatric.'

Honestly, sometimes I long for the bygone days, when people spoke politely to each other. You would never guess that my mother and Bert are fond of each other.

Everyone was too old, or too ill, or too pregnant to do any cooking (I developed a sudden ache in both wrists). So we ate bread and cheese for our Sunday dinner. Then, in the afternoon we took it in turns to teach Queenie to speak again.

I got her to say, 'A jar of beetroot please,' dead clearly. I might be a speech therapist when I grow up. I have got a definite flair for it. We got a taxi back home because my mother's ankles got a bit swollen. The taxi driver moaned because the distance was only half a mile.

Monday   November 8th

I was woken up at 3 a.m. by the sound of my mother crying.

She wouldn't say what was wrong, so after patting her on the shoulder I went back to bed.

I wish she'd let my dad come back. After all he *has* said he's sorry.

Tuesday   November 9th

Couldn't concentrate at school for worrying about my mother. Mr Lambert told me off for staring out of the window when I should have been writing about the future of the British Steel Industry.

He said, 'Adrian, you've only got three minutes to finish your essay.' So I wrote: 'In my opinion there *is* no future for the British Steel Industry, while the present government is in power.' I know I'll get into trouble, but I gave it in anyway.

Wednesday   November 10th

My mother has gone mad cleaning the house from top to bottom. She has taken all the curtains and nets down. Now anybody passing by in the street can look in and see our most intimate moments.

I was examining my spots in the living-room mirror tonight, when Mr O'Leary shouted from the street: 'There's a fine pimple on the back of your neck, don't miss that one out, boy.'

It's taken me fifteen years to appreciate the part that curtains have played in civilized English life.

Mr Brezhnev, the Russian Prime Minister, died today. World leaders have been sending lying telegrams to the Kremlin saying how sorry they are.

Thursday   November 11th
ARMISTICE DAY

When I got home from school my mother's little suitcase was missing from the hall. She was nowhere in the house, but I found a note on the biscuit tin. It said:

> Waters broke at 3.35. I am in the labour ward of the Royal Infirmary. Call a taxi. £5 note at bottom of spaghetti jar. Don't worry.
> Love, Mum
> P.S. Dog at Mrs Singh's.

Her writing looked dead untidy.

The taxi ride was a nightmare. I was struggling to get my hand free of the spaghetti jar all the way. The taxi driver kept saying, 'You should have tipped the jar upside down, you stupid bleeder.'

He parked outside the entrance to the hospital, and watched the jar versus my hand struggle in a bored sort of way. He said, 'I'll have to charge you waiting time.' A hundred years passed: then he said, 'And I can't change a five-pound note either.'

I was almost in tears by the time I managed to pull my hand free. I had a mental image of my mother calling for me. So I gave the taxi driver the fiver, and ran into the hospital. Found the lift and pressed the button which said 'Labour Ward.'

I emerged into another world. It looked like the space control centre at Houston.

A technician asked, 'Who are you?'

I said, 'I'm Adrian Mole.'

'And you've got permission to visit the labour ward?'

'Yes,' I said. (Why did I say yes? Why?)

'Room 13. She's being a bit stubborn.'

'Yes, she's a stubborn kind of person,' I said, and walked down the corridor. Doors opened and shut and I caught glimpses of women hooked up to gruesome-looking equipment. Moans and groans bounced around the shiny floors. I pushed the door of Room 13 open and saw my mother lying on a high bed reading *Memoirs of a Fox-hunting Man* by Siegfried Sassoon.

She looked pleased to see me and then asked why I'd brought the spaghetti jar into the hospital. I was halfway through telling her, when she screwed her face up and started singing 'Hard Day's Night.'

After a bit she stopped singing and looked normal. She even laughed when I got to the bit about the horrible taxi driver. After a bit a kind black nurse came in and said, 'Are you all right, honey?'

My mother said, 'Yes. This is Adrian.'

The nurse said, 'Put a mask and gown on, Adrian, and sit in a corner; it's going to be action stations soon!'

After about half an hour my mother was singing more and talking less. She kept grabbing my hand and crushing it. The nurse came back in and to my relief told me to go out. But my mother wouldn't let go of my hand. The nurse told me to make myself useful and time the contractions. When she'd gone I asked my mother what contractions were.

'Pains,' she said, between clenched teeth. I asked her why she hadn't had her back frozen to stop the pain. My mother said, 'I can't stand people fiddling around with my back.'

The pains started coming every minute, and my mother went barmy, and a lot of people ran in and started telling her to push. I sat in a far corner at the head end of my mother and tried not to look at the other end where doctors and nurses were clanging about with metal things. My mother was puffing and panting, just like she does at Christmas when she's blowing balloons up. Soon everyone was shouting, 'Push, Mrs Mole, push!' My mother pushed until her eyes nearly popped out. 'Harder,' they shouted. My mother went a bit barmy again, and

the doctor said, 'I can see the baby's head!'

I tried to escape then but my mother said, 'Where's Adrian? I want Adrian.'

I didn't like to leave her alone with strangers, so I said I'd stay. I stared at the beauty spot on my mother's cheek for the next three minutes, and I didn't look up, until I heard the black nurse say, 'Pant for the head.'

At 5.19 p.m. my mother had a barmy moment; then the doctor and nurses gave a sort of loud sigh, and I looked up and saw a skinny purple thing hanging upside down. It was covered in white stuff.

'It's a lovely little girl, Mrs Mole,' the doctor said, and he looked dead pleased, as if he were the father himself.

My mother said, 'Is she all right?'

The doctor said, 'Toes and fingers all correct.'

The baby started crying in a crotchety, bad-tempered way, and she was put on my mother's flatter belly. My mother looked at her as if she was a precious piece of jewellery or something. I congratulated my mother and she said, 'Say hello to your sister.'

The doctor stared at me in my mask and gown and said, 'Aren't you Mr Mole, the baby's father?'

I said, 'No, I'm Master Mole the baby's brother.'

'Then you've broken every rule in this hospital,' he said. 'I must ask you to leave. You could be rife with childish infectious diseases.'

So, while they stood around waiting for something called the placenta to emerge, I went into the corridor. I found a waiting-room full of worried-looking men, smoking and talking about cars.

(To be continued after sleep.)

At 6.15 I rang Pandora and told her the news. She did big squeals down the phone. Next I rang Grandma, who did big sobs.

Then I phoned Bert and Queenie, who threatened to come and see my mother. But I managed to put them off. Then I ran out of five pence pieces, so I called in to see my mum and sister.

Then went home. I walked around the empty house, trying to imagine sharing it with a little girl.

I put all my smashable possessions on the top shelf of my unit. Then went to bed. It was only 7.30 but for some reason I was dead tired. The phone woke me up at 8.15. It was my father gibbering about having a girl. He wanted to know every detail about her. I said she took after him. Half bald and angry-looking.

Friday   November 12th

The Russians chose their new leader today. He is called Andropov. I am a hero at school. The story has got round that I *delivered* the baby. The dinner lady in charge of chips gave me an extra big portion. Went to the hospital to see my female relations after school.

I am staying at Pandora's house. Over supper I gave them a blow-by-blow account of the birth. Halfway through Mr Braithwaite got up and left the table.

Saturday   November 13th

Pandora and I went to see my mother and the baby this afternoon. We had to fight our way through the crowd of visitors round her bed. For such a stubborn person she is certainly popular. The baby was passed around like an exhibit in a court room. Everyone said, 'Isn't she beautiful?'

The women said, 'Ooh it makes me feel broody!'

The men said, 'Small fingernails.'

Then Queenie and Bert arrived, so a space was cleared for Bert's wheelchair, and Queenie sat on the bed and squashed my mother's legs and it was dead chaotic. The nurses started looking efficient and bossy. A staff nurse said, 'You are only allowed two visitors to a bed.' Just then my grandma and father turned up. So everyone else was pleased to go and leave these two particular visitors at the bed.

Sunday   November 14th
REMEMBRANCE SUNDAY

My mother phoned me up to tell me that she is coming home at 10.30 tomorrow morning. She told me to make sure the heating is switched on. I asked if she wanted a taxi ordering. She said, 'No, your father has kindly offered to pick us up.'

Us! I am no longer an only child.

Watched the poppies falling on to the heads of the young kids in Westminster Abbey. My eyes started running: I think I've got a cold coming on.

Monday   November 15th

Skived off school. Mrs Singh and Mrs O'Leary came round early to tidy the house. I said I was perfectly capable, but Mrs O'Leary said: 'Sure, you're talking nonsense, child. How would a lump like you know how to make a house nice enough to pass the eagle eyes of a woman?'

At 11.15 I saw the bizarre sight of my father carrying his daughter down the front path. Followed by my thin purple-haired mother. I haven't got enough emotions to cope with all the complexities of my life. After going mad over the baby, Mrs Singh and Mrs O'Leary melted away and left my immediate family staring at each other. To break the tension I made a cup of tea.

My mother took hers to bed and I let mine go cold. My father hung about for a bit then went home to Grandma's.

The midwife came at 2.30. She did mysterious things to my mother in the privacy of the master bedroom. At 3.15 the midwife came downstairs and said my mother was suffering from after-baby blues caused by hormone trouble. She asked me who was looking after my mother. I said I was. She said, 'I see,' in a thin-lipped manner. I said, 'I am perfectly capable of pushing a Hoover around!'

She said, 'Your mother needs more support.'

So I took the pillows off my own bed and gave them to my mother. This act of kindness made my mother cry.

Tuesday   November 16th

Phoned the school secretary Mrs Claricoates and enquired about maternity leave. Scruton came on the line. He barked, 'If I don't see you in school tomorrow, Mole, I shall be severely displeased!'

The baby woke up five times in the night. I know, because I sat by her cot, checking her breathing every ten minutes.

My mother has stopped crying and started wearing mascara again.

Wednesday   November 17th

Mrs Singh and Mrs O'Leary are taking it in turns to look after my mother and sister. Pandora says I am beginning to be a bore about the baby. She says that my sister's feeding pattern isn't of great interest to her. How callous can you get?

Thursday   November 18th

My father was ironing baby clothes when I got home from school. He said, 'If you laugh, I'll kill you.' My mother was feeding the baby, with her feet on the dog's back. It was a charming domestic picture, only spoiled when my father put the ironing board away and went home to his other family.

Friday   November 19th

I asked my mother what she was going to call the baby.

She said, 'I can't think beyond the next feed – let alone decide on a name.'

I suggested we both make a list, so after the next feed we did.

My mother's	*Mine*
Charity	Tracy
Christobel	Claire
Zoe	Toyah
Jade	Diana
Frankie	Pandora

India	Sharon
Rosie	Georgina
Caitlin	
Ruth	

I only liked 'Rosie' and 'Ruth' out of my mother's list. She didn't like any in my list. She said, 'Pandora is a pretentious name!' I think it is the most evocative girl's name in the history of the world. Whenever I say it, or hear it, I get a bursting feeling behind my ribs.

Saturday   November 20th

My sister's name is Rosie Germaine Mole.

Everybody likes 'Rosie' but only my mother likes 'Germaine'. The registrar raised his eyebrows, and said, 'Germaine? As in *Female Eunuch*?'

My mother said, 'Yes, have you read it?' 'No, but my wife can't put it down,' he said, smoothing his unironed shirt.

We celebrated Rosie being on the official record sheet of Great Britain by going into a café, and having a meal. Rosie was in a baby sling squashed against my mother's chest. She was dead well-behaved. She only woke up when my mother dropped a warm chip on her head. After the meal, we caught a taxi home. My mother was too tired to walk to the bus stop.

Sunday   November 21st

My father came round with £25. He mooned over my mother while she was defrosting a shoulder of lamb under the hot tap. They started having an intense conversation about their future relationship. So I took the dog for a walk into the garden for a session of obedience training, but it was a waste of time. Our dog would have Barbara Woodhouse in tears.

Monday   November 22nd

We had to write a description of a person in English. So I wrote about Rosie.

Rosie

Rosie is about eighteen inches long, she has got a big head with fuzzy black hair in a Friar Tuck style. Unlike the rest of our family, her eyes are brown. She has got quite a good skin. Her mouth is extremely small, except when she is screaming. Then it resembles an underground cavern. She has got a wrinkled-up neck like a turkey's. She dresses in unisex clothes, and always wears disposable nappies. She lazes about all day in a carrycot and only gets out when it is time to be fed or changed. She has got a split personality; calm one minute, screaming like a maniac the next.

She is only eleven days old but she rules our house.

Tuesday   November 23rd

Rat fink Lucas phoned up tonight. My mother spoke to him for about ten minutes in a mumbling sort of way, as though she didn't want me to hear. But I certainly heard the last thing she said before she threw the phone across the hall. Because it was said at a high rate of decibels.

'ALL RIGHT – HAVE A BLOOD TEST!'

Perhaps Lucas thinks he's got a deadly blood disease. I hope he has.

Wednesday   November 24th

Mr O'Leary has gone to Ireland to vote in the Irish election, which is being held tomorrow. I admire his patriotism: but I can't understand why he doesn't live in Ireland all the time. I will ask him when he comes back. Mrs O'Leary is not so patriotic. She stayed at home and threw a party for somebody called 'Ann Summers'. My mother was invited but didn't go.

She said Ann Summers was responsible for getting her into her present mess.

I watched the O'Learys' front door all night but all I saw was just a load of middle-aged women giggling and clutching brown paper bags.

Thursday   November 25th

Nobody won in the Irish General Election. It was a draw.

Mr O'Leary was detained at East Midlands airport on suspicion of being a terrorist but he was let off with a warning and told not to bring Action Man accessories into the country again.

Friday   November 26th

I got a dead horrible shock when I came out of the school gate today. Stick Insect was waiting for me. She stood there rocking an old royal family pram which contained Brett and Maxwell. She looked like a refugee from a Second World War newsreel. Maxwell shouted, 'Hello brudder.' I thought he was talking to Brett, but no, the kid was talking to me! I shoved a bit of Mars bar into his mouth before he could show me up any more, and introduced Pandora to Stick Insect.

I said, 'My girl-friend, Pandora,' to Stick Insect; and, 'Mrs Doreen Slater,' to Pandora. The two women looked each other up and down in a split second, and then smiled in a false way.

'What perfect darlings,' said Pandora, looking in the pram.

'They're both little buggers,' Stick Insect whined. 'I'd never have had them if I'd known.'

'Known what?' said Pandora, pretending to be innocent.

'Known that they take your life over. Don't you have none,' she warned.

Pandora said, 'I hope I shall have six!'

'*And* be editor of *The Times*?' I said sarcastically.

'Yes,' said Pandora, 'and I shall do my own painting and decorating!'

'You wait,' said Stick Insect. 'You just wait.' It was like a gypsy's curse.

I asked S.I. why she'd waited for me, and she told me that my father was awful to live with, and that Grandma was worse.

I said, 'Well what can I do about it?'

Stick Insect said, 'I just wanted to get it off my chest!' (Flat). Then she wheeled the kids back to Grandma's.

I don't know a single sane adult. They are all barmy. If they are not fighting in the Middle East, they are dressing poodles in plastic macs or having their bodies deep frozen. Or reading the *Sun*, because they think it is a newspaper.

Saturday   November 27th

Changed my first nappy tonight.

Tomorrow I am going to try doing it with my eyes open.

Sunday   November 28th

How is it that my mother can change Rosie's yukky nappies and at the same time smile and even laugh? I nearly fainted when I tried to do it without a protective device (clothes peg). Perhaps women have got poorly developed nasal passages.

I wonder if research has been done into it? If I pass 'O' level Biology I may even do it myself.

Monday   November 29th

My mother's gone right off me since Rosie was born. She was never a particularly attentive mother – I always had to clean my own shoes. But just lately I have been feeling emotionally deprived. If I turn out to be mentally deranged in adult life, it will all be my mother's fault.

I'm spending most of the time reading in my room. I've just finished reading *To Sir with Love*. It's about a black teacher who is badly treated by white yobs. But by persevering, and being kind yet firm, he triumphs over them, and decides not to be an

engineer. I give it five out of ten. Which is not bad because I am very discriminating.

Tuesday   November 30th
ST ANDREW'S DAY

Made my Christmas present list out in order of preference.

> *Big present list*
> Word Processor (no chance)
> Colour Telly (portable)
> Amstrad Hi-Fi unit (for future record collections)
> Electronic typewriter (for poems)
> $\frac{3}{4}$-length sheepskin coat (for warmth and status)

> *Small present list*
> Pair of trousers (pegs)
> Adidas trainers (size ten)
> Adidas anorak (36" chest)
> Anglepoise lamp (for late-night poetry)
> Gigantic tin of Quality Street
> Solid gold pen set (inscribed A. Mole)
> Pair slippers
> Electric razor
> Habitat bath robe (like Pandora's dad's)

> *Things I always get whether I want them or not*
> *Beano* Annual
> Chocolate smoking set
> Pkt felt-tip pens
> False nose/glasses/moustache

I gave my mother the list, but she wasn't in the mood for talking about Christmas. In fact just mentioning Christmas put her in a bad mood.

Wednesday   December 1st

An emotion-packed phone call from Grandma: Stick Insect has taken Brett and Maxwell to stay with Maxwell's father, who has just come back from the Middle East, loaded with tax-free money and stuffed toy camels!

Apparently my father doesn't mind being deprived of his paternal rights and Maxwell's dad doesn't care that Stick Insect has had a baby in his absence. I am shocked. Am I to be the sole guardian of the little morality left in our society?

Thursday   December 2nd

Maxwell's dad, Trevor Roper, doesn't mind about Brett because he thinks Brett is the result of having faulty coitus interruptus!

Stick Insect is getting married to Mr Roper as soon as his divorce is through. It's no wonder the country is on its knees. I am seriously thinking about returning to the church. (Not to go to Stick Insect's wedding either.) I have made an appointment to see a vicar, Reverend Silver. I got him out of the Yellow Pages.

Friday   December 3rd

The vicar was mending his bike when I first saw him. He looked quite normal except that he was wearing a black dress.

He got up and gave me a bone-crushing handshake. Then he took me to his study and asked me what I wanted to see him about. I said I was worried about the disintegration of morals in modern life. He lit a cigarette with trembly hands, and enquired if I had asked God for guidance. I said I had stopped believing in God. He said, 'Oh God, not another one!' He talked for ages. It all boiled down to having faith. I said I hadn't got faith and asked him how to get it.

He said, 'You must have faith!' It was like listening to a stuck record. I said, 'If God exists how come He allows wars and famines and motorway crashes to happen?'

Rev. Silver said: 'I don't know, I lie awake wondering that myself.'

Mrs Silver came in with two mugs of Nescafé, and a box of Mr Kipling's iced fancies.

She said, 'Derek, your Open University thing is starting in ten minutes.'

I asked the Rev. Silver what he was studying. He said, 'Microbiology. You know where you are with microbes.'

I said goodbye and wished him luck in his change of career. He told me not to despair, and showed me out into the mad, bad, world. It was cold and dark and some yobs were throwing chips about in the street. I went home feeling worse than ever.

Saturday   December 4th

I am having a nervous breakdown. Nobody has noticed yet.

Sunday   December 5th

Went to see Bert; he is my last hope. (Pandora failed me. She blamed my mental state on my being a meat eater.) I said, 'Bert, I am having a breakdown! Bert said that he had had a breakdown in the first World War. He said his was caused by seeing thousands of dead men and being constantly afraid for his life. He asked what mine was caused by.

I said, 'The lack of morals in society.'

Bert said, 'You daft bugger, what you need is a good stint of hard work. You can start on the washing up.'

When I'd finished Queenie made me a cup of tea, and a pile of crab paste sandwiches. While I ate I watched *Songs of Praise* on the television. The church was full of happy-looking people all singing their hearts out.

How come they've got faith and I've not? Just my luck!

Monday   December 6th

I was woken up at 1 a.m., 2.30 a.m. and 4 a.m. by Rosie screaming.

I got up at 6 a.m. and listened to a farming programme on Radio Four. Some old rustic gasbag was drivelling on about geese farming in Essex. At 8.30 I went into my mother's room, to ask for my dinner money and found Rosie fast asleep in my mother's bed. This is strictly forbidden by the baby books.

I checked that Rosie could breathe properly, then, after taking three pounds out of my mother's purse, I went to school and tried to behave normally.

Tuesday   December 7th

Queenie died at 3 o'clock this morning. She had a stroke in her sleep. Bert said that it was a good way to go, and I am inclined to agree with him. It was strange to go into Bert's house and see Queenie's things all over the place. I still can't believe she is dead and that her body is in the Co-op Funeral Parlour.

I didn't cry when my mother told me the news, in fact I felt like laughing. It wasn't until I saw Queenie's pot of rouge standing on the dressing table, that tears leaked out. I didn't let Bert see me crying, and he didn't let me see him crying. But I know he has been. There are no clean hankies left in his drawer.

Bert doesn't know what to do about death certificates, and funeral arrangements etc. So Pandora's father came round to do all the death paperwork.

Wednesday   December 8th

Bert has asked me to write a poem to put in the Deaths column of the local paper.

10 p.m. I am terrified. In fact I have got writer's block.

11.30 p.m. Unblocked. Finished poem.

Thursday   December 9th

The following announcements appeared in the paper tonight:

BAXTER, Maud Lilian (Queenie). Passed away peacefully at home on 7th December 1982. To the best girl that ever was. Bert, Sabre and Adrian.

> White face, red cheeks.
> Eyes like crocus buds.
> Hands deft and sure, yet worked to gnarled roots.
> A practical comfortable body, dressed in young colours.
> Feet twisted, but planted firmly on the ground.
> A sure soft voice, with a crackly sudden laugh.
> Her body is lifeless and cold,
> But the memory of her is joyful and as warm as a rockpool in August.

Funeral service and cremation, Monday 13th December at 1.30 p.m. at Gilmore's crematorium. Floral tributes to Co-operative funeral service.
Written with love, from Adrian, on the instructions of Mr Bertram Baxter.

BAXTER, Queenie: Sadly missed, Pauline and Rosie Mole.

BAXTER, Maud Lilian:
> The parting was so sudden.
> We sit and wonder why.
> The saddest thing of all,
> Is that we never said goodbye.

From your grieving son, Nathan, and your daughter-in-law, Maria and Jodie and Jason, grandchildren.

BAXTER, Queenie: Adieu Queenie, Mr and Mrs Braithwaite and Pandora.

BAXTER, Queenie:
> Always a smile and a kindly word.

She'd never pass on the things she heard.
She bore her troubles with never a moan.
To every stray dog she would give a bone.

God Bless Queenie. From your friends at the 'Evergreens'.

BAXTER, Queenie: Life is a struggle in search of a vision. You have found your vision we hope. From your friends, the Singh Family.

BAXTER, Queenie: Words can't express how much I will miss my old pal. Your neighbour, Doris.

BAXTER, Queenie: Deepest sympathy, from John the milkman.

BAXTER, Queenie: We have lost a dear old friend. Julian and Sandy, at the 'Jolie Madame' Hair Salon.

BAXTER, Queenie: A sad loss. May and George Mole.

BAXTER, Queenie: I'll miss you, Queenie. Betty in the sweet shop and her husband, Cyril, and children Carol and Pat.

My tribute to Queenie has caused a stir. People have said it's in bad taste, and have complained that it doesn't rhyme. Must I live amongst uneducated peasants – for the rest of my life? I long for the day when I buy my first studio flat in Hampstead. I will have a notice on my door: 'NO HAWKERS TRADERS OR PHILISTINES.'

Friday   December 10th

Mr Braithwaite is very worried about Queenie's funeral. The cheapest he can arrange will cost £350. (Plain coffin, one hearse, one mourners' car.) But Queenie's funeral insurance is

only worth £30. She took it out in 1931 when £30 would buy you: a fancy coffin, two teams of black horses with plumes, a funeral tea, and a gang of top-hatted attendants. The death grant the government gives you is no help. It doesn't buy a brass coffin nail.

The only solution is for Bert to take out hire-purchase and have Queenie's funeral on the never-never.

Saturday   December 11th

The finance company have turned down Bert's request for a loan. They say he is too old at nearly ninety, so it looks like Queenie will have to be buried by Social Security (grey van, plywood coffin, ashes put in a jam jar).

Bert is dead upset. He said, 'I wanted my girl to go out properly!' I spent all night phoning around to everyone who knew Queenie, getting them to donate money. I was called a saint several times.

Sunday   December 12th

My mother has gone out with Mrs Singh, Mrs O'Leary and her women's group to have a picnic on Greenham Common. She has taken Rosie, so the house is dead peaceful.

I played my 'Toyah' records at full volume and had a bath with the door open.

10.02 p.m. I have just seen the Greenham women on the telly! They were tying babies' bootees on to the wire surrounding the missile base. Then they held hands with each other. The newscaster said that 30,000 women were there. The dog was sulking because my mother had gone out for the day. It didn't understand that she was miles away safeguarding its future.

They got back safely. The Women's group came back to our house. They talked about female solidarity, while I served them coffee and tuna sandwiches. I felt excluded from the conversation so I went to bed.

2.00 a.m. Just woken up by Mr Singh and Mr O'Leary banging

on our door demanding entrance. I got up and explained to them that there were about twenty women in our living room. Mr O'Leary said, 'Tell Caitlin to hurry up; I can't find my pyjamas.' Mr Singh said, 'Ask Sita to tell me how to work our electric kettle.'

I advised them to go home for their own safety.

Monday   December 13th

Queenie's funeral.
We dropped Rosie off at Mrs Singh's and walked round to Bert's bungalow. All the curtains in the street were shut out of respect for Queenie. The neighbours were out looking at the floral tributes, which were lined up alongside the little path to the front door. Bert was sitting in his wheelchair wearing his wedding suit. Sabre was sitting by his side. My mother gave Bert a kiss.

Bert said, 'I don't like to think about her lying in an unheated coffin, she never did like the cold.'

My mother acted as hostess because none of Queenie's relations came. (Queenie quarrelled with them because they disapproved when she married Bert.)

The mourners' cars arrived so me and the Co-op men carried Bert out to the leading car, then me and my mother and Doris from next door, and Mr and Mrs Braithwaite and Pandora sat in the leading car. The second car filled up with less important mourners and we set off very slowly to Gilmore's Crematorium. As we passed the cemetery gates, an old man took his hat off and bowed his head. Bert said that the old man was a stranger. I was very touched by this gesture of respect.

My mother and father sat together in the chapel, briefly united. Me and Pandora sat either side of Bert. He said he wanted to have 'young 'uns' around him.

The service was short; we sang Queenie's favourite carol, 'Away in a Manger', and her favourite song, 'If I ruled the World.'

Then, while the organ played sad music, the coffin started

sliding towards purple curtains around the altar. When the coffin reached the curtains Pandora whispered, 'God, how perfectly barbaric.'

I watched with horror as the coffin disappeared. Bert said, 'Tara old girl' and then Queenie was burnt in the oven.

I was so shocked, I could hardly walk up the aisle. Pandora and I both looked up when we got outside. Smoke was pouring out of the chimney, and was carried away by the wind. Queenie always said she wanted to fly.

I suppose there is a sort of logic to life and death. Rosie was born and so Queenie had to make way for her. The funeral tea was held at Pandora's house; it was a very jolly affair. Bert held up well, and even cracked a few jokes. But I noticed that whenever I mentioned Queenie's name, people looked away, and pretended not to hear. So Bert is on his own again, and will need more looking after than ever!

How will I cope? I've got my 'O' levels in June.

Tuesday   December 14th

It was on Radio Four that the government is spending a billion pounds on buying war equipment. Yet one of our science laboratories at school is closing down after Christmas, because our school can't afford to pay a new teacher. Poor old Mr Hill is retiring after thirty years of sweating over the Bunsen burners. He will be sadly missed. He was dead strict but dead fair with it. He was never sarcastic and seemed to listen to what you were saying. Also he gave out mini Mars bars for good work.

Wednesday   December 15th

We put the Christmas tree up tonight. It had gone a bit rusty, but I tied tinsel round the worst bits. My mother insisted on hanging up the decorations I made when I was a little kid. She said they had sentimental value for her. It looked OK when all the flashy balls and bad-taste angels were bunged on it.

I picked Rosie up and showed her the finished tree, but I

can't say she was overjoyed. In fact she just yawned. The dog, on the other hand, had one of its mad fits, and had to be restrained with a rolled-up *Guardian*.

Thursday   December 16th

Bought a pack of cheap Christmas cards from Cherry's, but didn't write in them. I will wait and see who sends me one first.

Friday   December 17th

The school's internal Christmas post service is as bad as the GPO's. I posted Pandora a card before assembly but she still hadn't had it by the end of the last lesson.

I will find out which first-years were on Elf duty today, and severely rebuke them.

Saturday   December 18th

Courtney has made £150 in tips from his post round. He is spending it on a weekend in Venice. He says that Christmas in Venice is an experience that everyone should have at least once in their lives. I wish I could have that experience. Courtney said that English canals are not a patch on Venetian ones.

Sunday   December 19th

Today Rosie Germaine Mole smiled for the first time. The recipient of the smile was the dog.

My father rang to ask what we are doing for Christmas. My mother said, 'The usual seasonal things, George: eating turkey, getting drunk, buying replacement bulbs for the fairy lights.'

My father said, 'Mother and me will be having *a quiet time, on our own, alone. Just the two of us. Away from our nearest and dearest.*'

My mother said, 'It sounds divine. Well I must dash. A crowd of pre-Christmas revellers have just turned up with the champagne.'

This was a complete and utter lie. It was only me coming into the room with a cup of cocoa.

Monday   December 20th

We break up tomorrow. So the school has gone a bit wild. The girls are doing no work at all, they just sit around the classrooms counting how many Christmas cards they've received from each other, and writing out hundreds more. The Elf postal service is being swamped.

I haven't sent any cards at all yet. I'm still waiting to see if anybody sends me one.

Tomorrow is the day of the school concert. It will be the first year I have had nothing to do. My mother is glad because it means she won't have to go.

Tuesday   December 21st

Last day of school
Thank God! I got seven Christmas cards. Three tasteful. Four in putrid taste and printed on flimsy rubbish paper that won't stand up. On receipt I quickly wrote out seven cards and gave them to a passing elf. Mr Golightly, director of the Christmas play, *The Importance of Being Earnest Christmas Show*, was very irritable today when I wished him good luck for tonight. He said, 'Thanks to your abdication, Adrian, I have got a midget playing Ernest.' (Peter Brown, whose mother smoked throughout her pregnancy!)

I'm glad I did abdicate from my role, because the play was a complete fiasco. Lady Bracknell forgot to say, 'A handbag?' And Peter Brown stood behind a chair so that the audience only saw the top of his head. Simone Bates, as Gwendoline, was quite good but what a shame her costume didn't hide her tattoos! The other parts are just not worth writing about.

The best thing in the show was the scenery. I congratulated Mr Animba, the woodwork teacher, on his dedication. He said, 'Do you think anybody noticed that it was adapted from the *Peter Pan* scenery of three years ago?' I assured him that nobody

had complained that the view from the french windows was of a palm-fringed island.

Mr Golightly was nowhere to be seen at the end of the play. Somebody told me that he had run from the wings shortly before the end, saying he had to visit his mother in hospital.

The best thing about the evening was the interval when Pandora played her viola in the refreshment room.

Wednesday   December 22nd

Drew £15 out of my Building Society today.

I know it's a lot but I've got an extra person to buy for: Rosie.

9.30 p.m. Forgot that Queenie isn't here any more. I needn't have been so extravagant. My memory!

Thursday   December 23rd

Made a list and went to Woolworth's, as they have got a good selection of festive gifts.

Dog	False bone	(£1.25)
Pandora	Solid gold chain	(£2.00)
Mother	Egg Timer	(About £1.59)
Rosie	Chocolate Santa	(79p)
Bert	20 Woodbines	(£1.09)
Nigel	He gets nothing this year	His best friend is now Clive Barnes
Father	Festive tin of anti-freeze	(£1.39)
Grandma	Gift pack of dusters	(£1.29)
Auntie Susan	Hankie Set	(99p)
Sabre	Dog Comb	(£1.29)

Woolworth's was swarming with last-minute shoppers, so I had to queue for half an hour at the checkout till. Why do people wait to do their shopping until there are only two days left before Christmas?

I couldn't get on a bus home because of the stupid lemmings.

Went to the 'Off the Streets' Youth Club party with Pandora. Nigel caused a scandal by dancing with Clive Barnes who was wearing lipstick and mascara!

Everyone was saying that Nigel is gay, so I made sure that everyone knew that he is no longer my best friend. Barry Kent smuggled two cans of 'Tartan' bitter through the fire doors. His gang of six shared them, and got leglessly drunk. At the end of the party Rick Lemon put 'White Christmas' by some old crumblie on the record deck and all the couples danced romantically together. I told Pandora how much I adored her and she said, 'Aidy, my pet, how long will our happiness last?'

Trust Pandora to put a damp cloth on everything. Saw her home. Kissed her twice. Went home. Fed dog. Checked Rosie's pulse. Went to bed.

Friday   December 24th
CHRISTMAS EVE

My mother is being kept a prisoner by Rosie; so I have had to do all the Christmas preparations. I was up at 7.30 queuing in the butcher's for a fresh turkey, pork joint, and sausage meat.

By 9 a.m. I was in the queue at the greengrocer's: 3 lbs sprouts, 24 tangerines, 2 lbs mixed nuts, 2 bunches of holly (make sure they have berries), salad (don't forget green pepper), 2 boxes of dates (get those with camel on lid), 3 lbs of apples (if no Cox's get G. Smith), 6 lbs potatoes (check each one for signs of sprouting).

By 11.15 I was in the launderette washing and drying the loose covers off the three-piece suite.

2 p.m. saw me at the grocer's with a long list, and Rosie's pram outside to cart everything home. £2.50's worth of Stilton (make sure good blue colour, firm texture), 2 boxes sponge fingers, red and yellow jelly . . . tin of fruit salad. . . . It went on for ever.

At 4.10 p.m. I was struggling into Woolworth's front doors, and trying to fight my way to the fairy-light counter. At 4.20 I got to the counter only to find empty shelves and other desperate

people swapping rumours: 'Curry's have got some lantern style', 'Rumbelow's have got two packets of the "star type"', 'Habitat have got the High Tech styles but they're pricey!'

I went to all the above shops and more, but at 5 p.m. I admitted defeat and joined the long queue at the bus stop.

Drunken youths covered in 'crazy foam' and factory girls wearing tinsel garlands paraded around the town singing carols. Jesus would have turned in his tomb.

At 5.25 I had a panic attack and left the queue and rushed into Marks and Spencer's to buy something.

I was temporarily deranged. A voice inside my head kept saying: 'Only five minutes before the shops shut. Buy! Buy! Buy!'

The shop was full of sweating men buying women's underwear. At 5.29 I came to my senses, and went back to bus stop. Just in time to see the bus leaving. I got home at 6.15 after buying a packet of fairy lights from Cherry's shop which is just around the corner from our house.

My mother has made the lounge look especially nice (she'd even dusted the skirting board) and when the new fairy lights were switched on, and the fruit arranged, and the holly stuck up etc, it looked like a room on a Christmas card. Me and my mother had a quick drink before Bert arrived in an Age Concern car, driven by a kind volunteer.

We settled him in front of the telly with a beetroot sandwich and a bottle of brown ale, and we went into the kitchen to start the mincepies and trifles.

1 a.m. Just got back from the Midnight Service. It was very moving (even for an atheist), though I think it was a mistake to have a live donkey in the church.

2 a.m. Just remembered, forgot to buy nutcrackers.

Saturday   December 25th
CHRISTMAS DAY

Got up at 7.30.

Had a wash and a shave, cleaned teeth, squeezed spots then

went downstairs and put kettle on. I don't know what's happened to Christmas Day lately, but something has. It's just not the same as it used to be when I was a kid. My mother fed and cleaned Rosie, and I did the same to Bert. Then we went into the lounge and opened our presents. I was dead disappointed when I saw the shape of my present. I could tell at a glance that it didn't contain a single microchip. OK a sheepskin coat is warm but there's nothing you can *do* with it, except wear it.

In fact after only two hours of wearing it, I got bored and took it off. However, my mother was ecstatic about her egg timer; she said, 'Wow, another one for my collection.' Rosie ignored the chocolate Santa I bought her. That's 79 pence wasted! *This is what I got:*

> $\frac{3}{4}$ length sheepskin coat (out of Littlewoods catalogue)
> *Beano* Annual (a sad disappointment, this year's is very childish)
> Slippers (like Michael Caine wears, although not many people know that)
> Swiss army knife (my father is hoping I'll go out into the fresh air and use it)
> Tin of humbugs (supposedly from the dog)
> Knitted Balaclava helmet (from Grandma Mole. Yuk! Yuk!)
> *Boys' Book of Sport* (from Grandma Sugden: Stanley Matthews on cover)

I was glad when Auntie Susan and her friend Gloria turned up; at 11 o'clock. Their talk is very metropolitan and daring; and Gloria is dead glamorous and sexy. She wears frilly dresses, and lacy tights, and high heels. And she's got an itsy-bitsy voice that makes my stomach go soft. Why she's friends with Auntie Susan, who is a prison warder, smokes Panama cigars and has got hairy fingers, I'll never know.

The turkey was OK. But would have been better if the giblets and the plastic bag had been removed before cooking. Bert made chauvinist remarks during the carving. He leered at

Gloria's cleavage and said, 'Give me a nice piece of breast.' Gloria wasn't a bit shocked, but I went dead red, and pretended that I'd dropped my cracker under the table.

When my mother asked me which part of the turkey I wanted, I said, 'A wing please!' I really wanted breast, leg, or thigh. But wing was the only part of the bird without sexual connotations. Rosie had a few spoons of mashed potato and gravy. Her table manners are disgusting, even worse than Bert's.

I was given a glass of Bull's Blood wine and felt dead sensual. I talked brilliantly and with consummate wit for an hour, but then my mother told me to leave the table, saying, 'One sniff of the barmaid's apron and his mouth runs away with him.'

The Queen didn't look very happy when she was giving her speech. Perhaps she got lousy Christmas presents this year, like me. Bert and Auntie Susan had a disagreement about the Royal Family. Bert said he would 'move the whole lot of 'em into council houses in Liverpool.'

Gloria said, 'Oh Bert that's a bit drastic. Milton Keynes would be more suitable. They're not used to roughing it you know.'

In the evening I went round to see Grandma and my father. Grandma forced me to eat four mincepies, and asked me why I wasn't wearing my new Balaclava helmet. My father didn't say anything; he was dead drunk in an armchair.

Sunday   December 26th
FIRST AFTER CHRISTMAS

Pandora and I exchanged presents in a candlelit ceremony in my bedroom. I put the solid gold chain round her neck, and she put a 70% wool, 10% cashmere, 20% acrylic scarf round my neck.

A cashmere scarf at fifteen!

I'll make sure the label can be seen by the public at all times.

Pandora went barmy about the solid gold chain. She kept looking at herself in the mirror, she said, 'Thank you, darling, but how on earth can you afford solid gold? It must have cost

you at least a hundred pounds!'

I didn't tell her that Woolworth's were selling them cheap at two pounds a go.

Monday   December 27th
BOXING DAY, HOLIDAY (UK EXCEPT SCOTLAND).
HOLIDAY (CANADA). BANK HOLIDAY (SCOTLAND).
HOLIDAY (REP OF IRELAND)

Just had a note handed to me from a kid riding a new BMX.

> Dear heart,
> I'm awfully sorry but I will have to cancel our trip to the cinema to see *ET*.
> I woke up this morning with an ugly disfiguring rash around my neck.
> Yours sincerely,
> Pandora
> P.S. I am allergic to non-precious metal.

Tuesday   December 28th

Walked up and down the High Street in my sheepskin coat and cashmere scarf. Saw Nigel in his new leather trousers posing at the traffic lights. He suggested we go to his house to 'talk'. I agreed. On the way he told me that he was trying to decide which sort of sexuality to opt for: homo, bi or hetero. I asked him which he felt more comfortable with. He said, 'All three, Moley.' Nigel could never make up his mind.

He showed me his presents. He had: a multi gym, Adidas football boots, a Mary Quant make-up hamper, and a unisex jogging suit.

Wednesday   December 29th

Danny Thompson has turned into a Rasta. I met him when I was walking up and down the High Street this morning. He asked me if I could play a musical instrument. I said, 'No.'

He said, 'Too bad, man, I needs a bass player real quick.'

I said I was surprised that a reggae band should need a double bass.

He did fancy hand-clapping and laughed and said, 'Bass *guitar*, what give out de rhythm.'

I said that my only contribution to the band could be as a lyricist.

He suggested I try writing a few songs and submitting them to the brothers. Then he gave me a complicated handshake and went off down the street with a springy step and with his blonde plaits bobbing up and down.

Thursday   December 30th
FULL MOON

Me, Mum, Rosie, Auntie Susan and Gloria went to Bridgegate Park today. Bert doesn't like fresh air so he stayed at home with the dogs and leftover Christmas food. We walked four boring miles. I walked behind Gloria so that I could watch her bum and legs properly. Auntie Susan and Gloria are going back to Holloway prison tonight. They will be sadly missed, they are so gay and vital. Bert is going back to his council bungalow. He will *not* be missed. He watches ITV all day and won't let anybody else hold Rosie.

Friday   December 31st

Bert has asked if he can stay on until New Year's Day. He said he can't face seeing the New Year in with only a Voluntary Social Worker's company. My mother agreed but she took me into the kitchen and whispered, 'Look, Bert's not living here for ever, Adrian. I can't look after a small baby and a geriatric at the same time!'

At eleven o'clock my father rang up to wish us all a Happy New Year. My mother's face went a bit blotchy and soft, and she invited him round for a drink.

At 11.15 rat fink Lucas rang from Sheffield, whining on about the fact that he was alone with a bottle of 'Johnnie

Walker'. My mother said, 'How appalling! You should have bought a decent brand – after all it is New Year's Eve.'

She looks dead nice again now that her figure is nearly back to normal. In fact after the phone calls she looked her old cocky self. My father crossed our doorstep at one minute to twelve, with a packet of 'Zip' firelighters (the nearest he could get to coal). Then, when the Scottish people on the telly went berserk at midnight, we all stood around Bert's wheelchair, holding hands and singing 'Auld Lang Syne'. Then we talked about Queenie and Stick Insect and said things like, 'Well I wonder what 1983 will bring us?'

Personally, nothing would surprise me any more. If my father announced that he was really a Russian agent or my mother ran away with a circus knife thrower, I wouldn't raise an eyebrow.

Pandora rang at 1 a.m. to say 'Happy New Year'. The Braithwaites' party sounded good. I wished I'd gone instead of being kind and staying at home. Went to bed rigid with fear. 1983 is my 'O' level year.

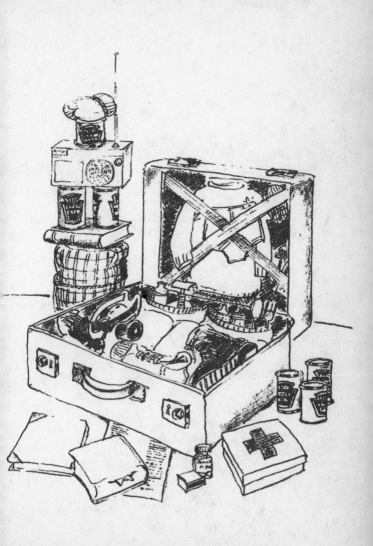

Saturday   January 1st 1983
NEW YEAR'S DAY

These are my New Year resolutions:

1. I will revise for my 'O' levels at least two hours a night.
2. I will stop using my mother's Buff-Puff to clean the bath.
3. I will buy a suede brush for my coat.
4. I will stop thinking erotic thoughts during school hours.
5. I will oil my bike once a week.
6. I will try to like Bert Baxter again.
7. I will pay my library fines (88 pence) and rejoin the library.
8. I will get my mother and father together again.
9. I will cancel the *Beano*.

Sunday   January 2nd

Took stock of my appearance today. I have only grown a couple of inches in the last year, so I must reconcile myself to the fact that I will be one of those people who never get a good view in the cinema.

My skin is completely disfigured, my ears stick out and my hair has got three partings and won't look fashionable whichever way I comb it.

Monday   January 3rd

Negotiations are going on between my parents for a return to their married state. My mother said, 'But how can it ever work, Adrian? There is so much to forget.' I suggested hypnosis.

Tuesday   January 4th

More negotiations behind closed doors. As he left, I asked my father for a report on the meeting. He said, 'No comment!' and got in his car.

Wednesday   January 5th

Negotiations have broken down.

I heard the sugar bowl crashing to the kitchen floor then raised voices. Then the door slamming.

Thursday   January 6th

A message was passed to an intermediary (me). That fresh negotiations would be welcomed. The message was passed on and the response was favourable, so it was left to me to arrange time, venue and baby-sitting details.

Friday   January 7th

The meeting took place in a Chinese restaurant at 8 p.m. Negotiations went on throughout the evening and were only adjourned when one party returned home to feed the baby.

Saturday   January 8th

Both parties have issued the following bulletin:

> It is agreed that Pauline Monica Mole and George Alfred Mole will attempt to live in mutual harmony for a trial period of one month. If during that time Pauline Monica Mole, hereafter known as P.M.M., and George Alfred Mole, hereafter known as G.A.M., break the following agreement, then the agreement shall be declared null and void, and divorce proceedings will automatically follow.

The Agreement
1. G.A.M. SHALL CHEERFULLY AND WITHOUT NAGGING OR REMINDING DO HIS RIGHTFUL SHARE OF HOUSEHOLD TASKS.
2. P.M.M. SHALL KEEP HER SIDE OF THE BEDROOM IN A HYGIENIC AND PRESENTABLE CONDITION.
3. BOTH PARTIES TO GO TO THE PUB AT SUNDAY LUNCHTIMES.

4. THE CHILDREN OF THE MARRIAGE, ADRIAN AND ROSIE MOLE, TO BE GIVEN FAIR AND EQUAL ATTENTION FROM BOTH PARENTS.

5. FINANCIAL MATTERS TO BE DISCUSSED EACH FRIDAY NIGHT AT 7 P.M.

6. A SEPARATE BANK ACCOUNT TO BE OPENED FOR P.M.M.

7. NEITHER PARTY TO INDULGE IN FLIRTATION, SEDUCTION OR ADULTERY WITH THE OPPOSITE SEX WITHOUT THE FULL KNOWLEDGE, OR CONSENT OF THE OTHER PARTY.

8. P.M.M. TO REPLACE CAP ON TOOTHPASTE AFTER USE.

9. G.A.M. TO WASH OWN HANDKERCHIEFS.

10. BOTH PARTIES TO HAVE UNLIMITED FREEDOM FOR THE PURSUIT OF HOBBIES, POLITICAL INTERESTS, DEMONSTRATIONS, AND SOCIAL INTERCOURSE OUTSIDE THE HOME.

11. G.A.M. TO THROW BOTH PAIRS OF CAVALRY TWILL TROUSERS AWAY.

12. P.M.M. WILL NOT CONSTANTLY HARP ON DOREEN SLATER EPISODE. G.M.M. WILL NOT DO THE SAME RE: LUCAS EPISODE.

Signed on this day the 8TH JANUARY 1983
Pauline Mole
George Mole
A. Mole, 1st Witness
Rosie Mole, 2nd Witness. Her mark. X

Sunday   January 9th

My father burnt his cavalry twills in the back garden today. As he poked the gobs of burning cloth he said, 'Well, it's the straight and narrow for me from now on.' I don't know whether he meant his life or his trousers.

Monday   January 10th

Lousy stinking school started today. Everybody was flashing their new calculators around. My sheepskin caused a bit of a stir wherever it went – and it went everywhere. It is far too valuable to leave in the cloakroom. Pandora and I held hands in assembly. But were spotted by Mr Scruton. He said, 'Keep your silly adolescent courtship rituals to outside school hours.' Pandora was still upset at break, but I comforted her in the Boys' toilets, by explaining that Mr Scruton was probably impotent, and it enraged him to see young lovers who were brimming with Eastern promise.

Tuesday   January 11th

Saw Roy Hattersley on the television tonight. He is putting weight on. He ought to go on a diet in case there's a General Election. The viewers don't like fat politicians. Look what happened to Churchill after the war. He was slung out because he got too fat. I know all this because we had a film of the Second World War in History today. I might be a historian if my memory improves.

Wednesday   January 12th

Nigel has formed a Gay Club at school. He is the only member so far, but it will be interesting to see who else joins. I noticed Brain Box Henderson hovering around the poster looking worried.

Thursday   January 13th

Mr Scruton has ordered the closure of the Gay Club, saying that he and the school governors couldn't sanction the use of the school gym for 'immoral purposes'. Nigel pretended to be innocent. He said, 'But sir, the Gay Club is for pupils who want to be frisky, frolicsome, lively, playful, sportive, vivacious or gamesome during the dinner break. What is immoral about gaiety?'

Mr Scruton said, 'Nigel, the word "Gay" has changed its meaning over the past years. It now means something quite different.'

Nigel said, 'What does it mean, sir?'

Scruton started sweating and messing about with his pipe, and not answering, so Nigel let him off the hook by saying: 'Sorry, sir, I can see that I will have to get an up-to-date dictionary!'

Friday   January 14th

Must go and see how Bert is getting on. God! I wish I'd never got involved with him; he is like an Ancient Mariner around my neck.

Saturday   January 15th

There is a new joke craze sweeping the school. In my opinion these so-called jokes are puerile. I watch in amazement as my fellow pupils roll helplessly in the corridors with tears of laughter coursing down their cheeks after relating them to each other.

1. Q. What do you call a man with a seagull on his head?
   A. Cliff.
2. Q. What do you call a man with a shovel in his head?
   A. Doug.
3. Q. What do you call a man without a shovel in his head?
   A. Douglas.
4. Q. What do you call an Irishman, who's been buried for fifty years?
   A. Pete.
5. Q. What do you call a man with fifty rabbits up his bum?
   A. Warren.

Come back, Oscar Wilde. Your country needs you.

Sunday   January 16th

6 p.m. My father put on his new straight-legged jeans today. He looks dead stupid in them. Talk about mutton dressed as lamb. He looks like stewing steak dressed as 'Flash Fry'.

I had to look after Rosie while my parents swanned down to the pub. I was also in charge of the pork and roast potatoes, and switching on the greens. I fed Rosie OK but it took ages to get her wind up. I patted her back for ages but it wasn't until I turned her upside down that she burped. I pretended not to notice that her nappy needed changing and acted surprised when my mother pointed out that there was a yukky smell in the room.

10 p.m. Now I come to a difficult entry. How exactly do I feel about my father's return home? It's been a week now and I've had plenty of time to think about it, but they've had these reconciliations before and they've ended in tragedy. So, I think I'll reserve my judgment until the slopping has stopped and they are back to normal.

12.15 a.m. Why didn't I go and see Bert? Why are you such a rat fink, Mole?

Monday   January 17th

Breakfast telly started today. I got up at 5.45 a.m. so I wouldn't miss history in the making. I made breakfast for me and the dog, and took it into the lounge. Normally cornflakes are banned from the lounge, on account of the odd one falling out of the bowl and sticking to the carpet, but I felt sure my mother wouldn't mind on this special occasion.

The dog fouled things up a bit by trampling into its bowl and scattering Pedigree Chum and Winalot into the shag pile. But I scraped the worst of the mess up with an empty fag packet, and we settled down to wait for 6.30. At 6.25 I woke my parents up by shouting loudly up the stairs that Breakfast Television was starting. My father shouted loudly down the stairs that he didn't want to see bloody Frank Bough at 6.30 a.m. in the

morning, and that he'd break my neck if I didn't turn the volume down.

Rosie woke up and started crying. I got the blame for that, and what with all the rowing and screaming I missed the very beginning. This is just my luck!

I enjoyed the Horoscopes, the News, the Celebrities and Frank Bough. He looks a steady sort of bloke. I wouldn't mind having a father like him. But best of all was Selina Scott, with her ravishing looks and quicksilver brain.

Courtney Elliott joined me in front of the screen at 7.45 a.m. He pronounced it 'lacking in intellectual fibre' and said he would stick to listening to Radio Four on his headset. I was late for school because Frank wasn't allowed to open the champagne until nearly nine o'clock!

I have written to the Director General to complain.

> Dear Sir,
> I wish to convey to you my congratulations on your new programme *Breakfast Time*. I saw the first episode and I thought it was a remarkable achievement considering. However, me and my fellow pupils were late for school, due to the late opening of the champagne.
>
> Either this shows a flagrant disregard for your teenage audience, or a woeful ignorance on your part, of the time I and my cohorts have to arrive at school in the morning.
>
> I suggest, Sir, that you do your research rather more thoroughly. Finally can I make a plea that in future episodes, any special items ie Ernest Hemingway chatting about his latest book, or Princess Diana having her horoscope read, will take place *before* 8.30 a.m. (except on Fridays when we don't have assembly).
>
> > Thanking you in anticipation of a reply,
> > Your most obedient servant,
> > A. Mole (aged 15 and 9 months)

Tuesday   January 18th

Lord Franks has published his report on the Falklands War,

but I will make no further comment until I have studied today's *Guardian* editorial on the matter.

10.30 p.m. Can't find *Guardian*: it's not in its usual place in the dog's basket.

Wednesday   January 19th

Found *Guardian* in dust-bin wrapped round yesterday's supply of disposable nappies. I made strong objections to my mother. Her feeble excuse was that she'd run out of plastic pedal bin liners.

Thursday   January 20th

Selina Scott is haunting my dreams: last night she was walking down our street selling cucumbers door to door. I bought half a dozen with a £50 note I had in my wallet. She smiled shyly and said, 'Prithee, how old are you, sire?' I answered, 'I be fifteen years, pretty maid.' Then the dog jumped on my face and woke me up.

I tried to tell my mother about my dream, but she refused to listen. She said, 'There is only one thing more deadly boring than listening to other people's dreams, and that is listening to other people's problems.'

Friday   January 21st

Last night Selina Scott and I were rowing the Atlantic single handed. Selina fell overboard and was swallowed by a dolphin. I swam into the dolphin's belly, and joined Selina: it was quite cosy. We had a glass of champagne then swam out and got back into the boat where we found Frank Bough teaching Pandora how to read out football results.

I told my father every detail of my dream (what Selina was wearing, etc) but I could tell he wasn't really interested. Now I know why people pay to go to psychiatrists. (They are the only people who will listen.)

Saturday   January 22nd

No Selina this morning, so I had to make do with going into town with Pandora, who wanted to buy a pair of neon pink legwarmers. After trekking round fifty shops while Pandora sneered at inferior pinks and rejected them all, I suggested we went for a cup of coffee. While I scraped the froth off, I confessed to Pandora how I felt about Selina. Pandora took it very calmly. She said, 'Yes, Selina Scott is to be congratulated, not many women could have borne the pain of so much plastic surgery!'

According to Pandora, Selina has had her nose, mouth, breasts, ears, and eyes remodelled by the surgeon's knife. Poor Selina has to spend three hours in the make-up chair in order to disguise the operation scars. Pandora went on to say, 'Of course she booked into the clinic under her real name, which is Edna Grubbe!'

I asked Pandora how she got her insight into the lives of the famous. Pandora stubbed her cigarette out and said, 'My family used to be on intimate terms with a high-up in the BBC.'

I asked who, a window-cleaner? But I said it quietly because Pandora had got into one of her moods. We resumed our search but none of the legwarmer shops had neon pink so Pandora is getting an 'Awayday' and going to London to buy some. She said, 'God how I hate the wretched provinces.'

Sunday   January 23rd

Rat fink Lucas rang up today. I told him that my mother was at the pub with my father. He asked me which pub, so I told him but instead of ringing off he asked me loads of questions about Rosie, and even asked me to bring her to the phone so that he could hear her gurgling. I told him that she was a late developer and was still at the screaming stage. Then Lucas said a weird thing: he said, 'That's my girl!'

My mother came home in a bad mood and my father came home in an even worse mood. It seems that my mother had left

the pub's darts match at a crucial point in order to answer a
telephone call.

Monday   January 24th

The water workers have gone on strike, so my father made us
all have a bath tonight. The dog included. Then he went
around collecting containers and filling them up. While he was
doing it he was whistling and looking cheerful. My father loves
a crisis.

Tuesday   January 25th

Fabulous! Amazing! Brilliant! Magic!
  Showers have been banned at school!
  The twice-weekly torture of displaying my inferior muscle
development is over. I hope the water workers prolong the
strike until I've left full-time education. They should stick out
for £500 a week, in fact.

Wednesday   January 26th

Courtney Elliot has offered to give me private tuition for my 'O'
levels. It seems he is a Doctor of Philosophy who left academic
life after a quarrel in a university common room about the
allocation of new chairs. Apparently he was promised a chair
and didn't get it.
  It seems a trivial thing to leave a good job for. After all, one
chair is very much like another. But then I am an existentialist
to whom nothing really matters.
  I don't care which chair I sit in.
  I am reading On the Road by Jack Kerouac.

Thursday   January 27th

Ken Livingstone was on the telly tonight, talking about his
triumph in getting the High Court to cut bus fares in London.
This led to me asking my parents for the bus fare to get to

school. I am tired out by the time I have walked a whole mile in the morning. My father said that he used to walk four miles to school and four miles back, through wind, rain, snow, hail, and broiling sun and fog.

I said sarcastically (though wittily), 'What strange climatic conditions prevailed in the Midlands in the nineteen-fifties!'

My father said, 'Weather was weather in those days. You wouldn't know proper weather if it came up and smashed you in the face.'

Friday   January 28th

I reminded my Father that the law about seat belts comes into force on Monday. He said, 'Nobody makes George Mole wear a baby harness.'

My mother said, 'A policeman will, so belt up!'

Saturday   January 29th

Bert Baxter rang to ask why I hadn't been round. I said I'd been too busy.

Bert said, 'Yes, too busy to visit an old lonely widower.'

I promised to go round tomorrow after dinner. Bert said, 'Dinner? What's that?'

I said, 'You remember, Bert, it's meat and three veg and gravy and stuff.'

Bert said that it was so long since he'd eaten properly that his vocabulary was suffering.

I asked him round for dinner tomorrow and told him that my father would give him a lift. But when I told my parents they went mad, and said that they'd arranged to visit some *properties* tomorrow and were planning to get a Chinese take-away.

Properties! Why didn't they consult me? After all, it is my 'O' level year and it is most important that I suffer no violent change, trauma or neurosis.

Sunday   January 30th

Spent Sunday afternoon reading the *News of the World* out loud to Bert. I was amazed at how many vicars are leaving their flocks and running away with attractive divorcees.

I also read him a few bits from *The Sunday Times* colour supplement, but Bert stopped me, saying, 'Do you think I'm interested in bleedin' Italian furniture, or "A day in the life" of a soddin' piano player?'

I said, 'I think you ought to keep up with modern cultural patterns!'

Bert said that whenever he heard the word 'culture' he reached for his bottle opener.

At 7 p.m. Bert's Age Concern volunteer turned up to take Bert to the pub. He is a thin, nervous-looking man called Wesley. Sabre growled and bared his horrible fangs when he came into the room. Bert said, 'Don't make any sudden moves, Wesley, Sabre's bite is worse than his bark.'

I couldn't resist showing off by throwing Sabre about and tickling his belly. I even did my party trick of putting my head in Sabre's mouth. I didn't leave it in long though; Sabre's breath stank of cheap dog meat.

After Wesley and Bert left I tidied up a bit. I found Bert and Queenie's wedding photo under Bert's pillow. Funny to think that old, smelly, unattractive people can be sentimental.

Monday   January 31st

On the way to school me and Nigel had a dead good time signalling to car drivers who had forgotten to put their seat belts on. Hardly any of them thanked us.

Tuesday   February 1st

The first cracks in the new marital alliance appeared today: an argument about money.

We are kept by the state in the style that the state wants to keep us, ie in poverty. My parents just can't cope with being

poor. It's all right for me because I'm used to it. I've never had more than three quid a week to call my own.

Wednesday   February 2nd

Lucas turned up on our doorstep halfway through *Coronation Street* demanding to see Rosie. My father said that Rosie was busy and couldn't be disturbed, but Lucas started shouting in his loud sing-song voice, so my father let him in to stop the neighbours talking.

My mother went dead pale under her Max Factor. Lucas said, 'Pauline, I want access to my child!'

My father's knees buckled a bit and he sat down on the arm of the settee to recover. He said weakly, 'Pauline, tell me that Rosie is mine!'

My mother said, 'Of course she's yours, George!'

Lucas took out a black 1982 diary and said, 'Pauline and I resumed our affair of the heart on February 16th 1982. However we did not consummate our new relationship until Sunday March 13th 1982, when Pauline came to a protest rally in Sheffield.'

My mother shouted, 'But I was wearing my new cap, I couldn't have got pregnant.'

My father said, 'Adulteress!'

'I'm not an adulteress,' my mother sobbed.

My father yelled, 'If the cap fits, wear it!'

'But I *did* wear it,' said my mother in anguish.

Lucas tried to put his arms around her but she Karate-chopped him on the back of the neck.

Everybody had forgotten I was there until I ran from the room, saying, 'I can't stand this eternal insecurity!'

As I ran to my room I passed Rosie in her cot. She was playing with her toes, unaware that her paternity was being settled downstairs.

Thursday   February 3rd

During the month of March 1982 it would seem that both my

parents were carrying on clandestine relationships, which resulted in the birth of two children. Yet my diary for that period records my childish fourteen-year-old thoughts and preoccupations.

I wonder, did Jack the Ripper's wife innocently write:

> *10.30 p.m.* Jack late home. Perhaps he is kept late at the office.
> *12.10 a.m.* Jack home covered in blood; an offal cart knocked him down.

Pandora is standing by me at this time of crisis. She is a true pillar of salt.

Friday   February 4th

I had to spend the day in matron's office due to feeling weak in the first lesson. (PE.)

She asked me if there was anything wrong at home. I started to cry and said that everything was.

She said, 'Adults have complicated lives, Adrian. It's not all staying up late and having your own door key!'

I said that *parents* ought to be moral and consistent and have principles.

She said, 'It's a lot to ask.'

I made her promise not to tell anyone that she'd seen me crying. She promised and kindly let me stay until my eyes had got back to normal.

Saturday   February 5th

Lucas continues to persecute us.

A solicitor's letter arrived today. He is taking us to court unless he is allowed access to Rosie.

Courtney Elliot suggested we find a good solicitor and get him to write a letter back saying that, unless Lucas stops his campaign, we will get an injunction out.

I don't know what it means, but it sounds dead threatening.

Sunday February 6th

I broke the silence of months and went to make my peace with Grandma. She was a bit frosty at first, but then she offered to make me some treacle toffee, so I knew I was forgiven.

She has bought a budgie called Russell. (Named after Russell Harty, her favourite person in the world after me.) She said, 'This little bird has given me more pleasure than my whole family put together, and what's more he listens and doesn't answer back.'

I didn't tell her about the Lucas affair. A further shock could kill her. She said that after the Stick Insect/Trevor Roper scandal, her hair fell out and has not grown back.

This explains why she was wearing her hat in the house.

Monday February 7th

Michael Heseltine has chickened out of a public debate on cruise missiles with CND. I expect he is scared of being shown up.

A similar thing is happening in our house; my father is refusing to talk to Pandora's mother, who is a marriage guidance counsellor.

Rosie is teething. She is getting through six bibs a day. Dribble hangs permanently from her mouth. She looks like a rabid dog.

Tuesday February 8th

Don't ask me how I am getting through the long school day. Just don't ask. I am walking around like a smiling robot. But my soul is weeping, weeping, weeping. If only the teachers knew that an unkind word from them brings tears to my eyes.

I am getting away with it by saying I've got conjunctivitis but it's a near thing sometimes.

The trial period is up today.

1 a.m. The two parties have agreed on an extension.

Wednesday   February 9th

The racehorse Shergar has been kidnapped by the IRA. Pandora seems more concerned about the horse's troubles than mine. I said, 'Haven't you got things out of perspective Pandora?'

She said, 'No, Shergar is highly bred and extremely sensitive. He must be suffering terribly.'

I don't know who to turn to for help. I might run away to London.

Thursday   February 10th

I've changed my mind about going to London.

According to *The Guardian* lead pollution is sending the cockneys who live there mad.

Friday   February 11th

We have got a solicitor called Cyril Hill. He has written a stern letter to rat fink Lucas, warning him to lay off our family.

The letter cost us £20.

Saturday   February 12th

The atmosphere at home is as thick as treacle, so I went to see Bert. I could hardly get in the door for Voluntary Social Workers, queuing up to be given their orders. None of them wanted to attend to Sabre's needs, however, so I mucked his kennel out and brushed his coat and then took him for his daily prowl round the recreation ground.

Barry Kent and his gang were there – tying the swings in knots, but with Sabre by my side I felt confident enough to have a go on the slide.

On the way back I passed several Alsatians and their male owners; perhaps it was a coincidence but *every* owner was practically a midget. Their Alsatians came up to their waists. I don't know what it means. But it must mean something.

Sunday February 13th

It's Valentine's Day tomorrow. I think I'll have the day off school. I can't stand being the only kid in my class who doesn't come into the classroom with a fistful of garish cards, and a self-congratulatory smile. I'll know I'll get one from Pandora, but she doesn't count; I've been going out with her for over a year.

Monday February 14th
ST VALENTINE'S DAY

Got four cards: one from Pandora, one from Grandma, one from my mother and one from Rosie.

Big, big deal!

I got Pandora a Cupid card and a mini pack of 'After Eights'. Lucas sent one to Rosie. My parents didn't bother this year, they are saving their money to pay for the solicitor's letter.

Tuesday February 15th
SHROVE TUESDAY

Pandora is not speaking to me because I absent-mindedly wrote 'Best Wishes' in her Valentine's card. She said, 'It's symptomatic of our decaying relationship, Adrian.'

I think she could be right. I'm going off her. She is too clever by half. My mother was too busy with Rosie to make pancakes, so I had a go. I don't know why my father went so mad, the kitchen ceiling needed decorating anyway.

Wednesday February 16th
ASH WEDNESDAY

Today is my parents' special day.

They are getting through thirty fags a day each. If Social Security hear about it they will get done and quite rightly!

Thursday   February 17th

I wrote a poem on the toilet wall at school today.

I thought it was a good way of getting a bit of political consciousness over to my moronic fellow pupils.

> *The Future*
> What future is there for the young?
> What songs are waiting to be sung?
> There are no mountains left to climb,
> No poetry without a rhyme.
> No jobs to go to after school.
> We divide and still they rule.
> They give us Job Creation Schemes.
> When what we want are hopes and dreams.
>   A. MOLE

Friday   February 18th

I was sent to see the headmaster today. He has found out about my toilet poem. I asked him how he knew I'd written it. He said, 'You signed it, idiot boy.' I have been suspended for a week.

Saturday   February 19th

Barry Kent and his gang called for me today. Kent said, 'We're going down town, you can come if you like!'

I was feeling a bit nihilistic so I went.

Sunday   February 20th

Hung around the deserted shopping centre with Barry Kent and the lads. I feel a curious affinity with the criminal classes. I am beginning to understand why Lord Longford (another noted intellectual) spends his time hanging around prisons.

Barry graciously gave me permission to call him 'Baz'.

Monday February 21st
WASHINGTON'S BIRTHDAY OBSERVANCE

Baz took me home and introduced me to his family today.

Mrs Kent said, 'Ain't you the lad what's 'ad all the scandal?'

I said, 'Yeah that's me, but so what?'

Mrs Kent said, 'That's no way to talk, young man.'

Mr Kent said, 'You keep a civil tongue in your head. That's my wife you're talking to.' I immediately apologized and remembered my manners. In fact I got up and offered Mrs Kent the unbroken chair.

The Kent children were swarming about in the living room, watching a television programme about the population explosion. A lurid coloured photo of Clive Kent in his army uniform stood on top of the radiogram. I asked how he was. Mrs Kent said, 'He's in an army hospital: his nerves is shot to pieces after the Falklands.'

I had a nice tea with the family; chip sandwiches with tomato sauce, and once I'd got used to the funny smell in the house I was able to relax for the first time in weeks.

Tuesday February 22nd

A note from Pandora:

> Adrian,
> As you seem to prefer the company of louts and anti-social drop-outs, I think it best if we finish. You have chosen to tread a different path from the one I intend to make my way on in the world.
> Thank you for the good times.
> Pandora Braithwaite

Wednesday February 23rd

Today I drew some money out of my Building Society account, and bought my first pair of Doc Marten's. They are bully-boy brown and have got ten rows of lace holes.

They add an inch to my height.

Thursday   February 24th

Spent the early part of the evening standing outside the off-licence with the gang. I made witty remarks about passing girls and made the gang laugh. They have started calling me 'Brains'. Baz has hinted that I have got leadership qualities.

Friday   February 25th

Mrs Kent has decided to have some new furniture, so the gang went to the rubbish tip to see what we could find. We came back with two almost unbroken kitchen chairs, a wicker linen basket, and a fireside rug. We are going back tomorrow with Rosie's pram to fetch a washing machine with mangle attachment.

Mrs Kent was very pleased with our haul: she said, 'It's a crying shame what folks chuck away!' Mr Kent lost his job two months ago, when the dairy closed down. He looked a bit ashamed when we brought the new furniture in. I heard him say to his wife, 'For better or worse, eh, Ida?'

Saturday   February 26th

I borrowed the pram OK but unfortunately Rosie was in it. She had to be taken out and carried for our journey back from the rubbish tip.

But she was a good kid and didn't cry once. Mrs Kent was overjoyed with her new washing machine. It looked OK when it had been wiped down. Mr Kent unscrewed the faulty motor, and started cleaning it down on the hearth rug, and Mrs Kent didn't murmur! My mother would have gone beserk. She won't let my father fill his lighter in the lounge.

Sunday   February 27th

Good news. The washing machine is working. There was a line of grey nappies on Mrs Kent's washing line today. I told her about 'Ariel' washing powder and she said, 'I'll buy some tomorrow when I get my family allowance.'

Monday February 28th

Rosie has got her first tooth. My index finger is still bleeding.

Tuesday March 1st

Spent the evening outside the Chinese chip shop chucking prawn crackers about with the gang. I haven't read a book for ages. Instead of reading about life I am living it.

Wednesday March 2nd
ST DAVID'S DAY

We are being persecuted by the police!

Tonight, as we were messing about in the shopping precinct, a police patrol car went by dead slowly, and the driver *looked* at us.

Talk about a police state!

Thursday March 3rd

The community policeman, PC Gordon, has been to see my parents, to warn them that I am running wild with a notorious gang. He is calling round tomorrow to give me a lecture on responsible citizenship.

Friday March 4th

PC Gordon is the sort of bloke you can't help liking. He is thin and jolly and he calls everybody 'Bucko'. But he said things like: 'You're obviously a clever lad, Adrian;' and: 'You're from a good family,' (Ha!); and 'Kent and his gang are no-hopers, they'll do you no favours.'

He asked me why I had suddenly gone off the rails. I said that I was an existentialist nihilist.

He said, 'Lads usually say they get into trouble because they're bored.'

I smiled cynically and said, 'Yes existential nihilism is just

one step further.' I could tell he was impressed by my vocabulary.

Later on my parents came in and used clichés like: 'He's a good lad at home' (my father); and: 'Barry Kent has led him astray' (my mother).

When he'd gone I polished my boots and went to bed with the dog.

Saturday   March 5th

Grandma rang and said that it was all round the Evergreens that I was 'keeping bad company'. She made me go round for tea. I didn't want to go, but there is something about Grandma's voice that makes you obey orders so I went.

While Grandma toasted crumpets on the electric coal fire she told me that my father had been in trouble with the police in 1953. She said, 'He got caught scrumping apples. The shame nearly killed me and your poor dead Grandad.'

I asked if my father had continued his criminal career.

She said, 'Yes, in fact he went from bad to worse, he went on to scrump pears and plums.'

I was curious to know how my father had been persuaded from taking up a life of crime. Grandma said, 'Your Grandad gave him a good thrashing with the buckle end of his belt.' Poor Dad! It explains why he is full of inner rage.

Sunday   March 6th

Being in a gang is not as exciting as I thought it would be. All we do is hang around shopping precincts and windy recreation grounds. Sometimes I long to be in my bedroom, reading, with the dog at my side.

Monday   March 7th

Just got back after a cold boring night of shouting in quiet streets. Barry Kent tipped a rubbish bin over for a laugh, but in fact it wasn't very funny and I had to force myself to guffaw with

the others in the gang. Barry Kent said, 'If it wasn't for me, my Uncle Pedro would lose his job!' His Uncle Pedro is a street cleaner.

After Barry went home I picked the broken glass up and replaced it in the bin. I wouldn't like a little kid to fall on it.

Tuesday   March 8th

There was a very unpleasant incident tonight.

Barry Kent shouted horrible names at two of the Singh kids. I said, 'Oh lay off em eh, Baz, they're all right!'

Barry sneered and said, 'I 'ate anyone who ain't English.'

I reminded him about his Uncle Pedro and he said, 'Except Spaniels.'

I can't go on leading this double life for much longer.

Wednesday   March 9th

I have decided not to take my 'O' levels. I am bound to fail them anyway so why waste all that neurosis in worrying? I'll need all the neurosis I can get when I start writing for a living.

Thursday   March 10th

The first page of my new novel:

> *Precinct by A. Mole, aged 15 years 11 months*
> Jake Butcher closed his eyes against the cruel wind that whistled over the paving slabs of the deserted shopping precinct. His cigarette dropped with a curse from his lips. 'Damn,' he expectorated.
>
> It was his last cigarette. He ground the forlorn fag under the sole of his trusty Doc Marten's boot. He dug both fists into the womb-like pockets of his anorak, and with his remaining hand he adjusted the fastening on his Adidas sports bag.
>
> Just then a sudden shaft of bright sunlight illuminated the windows of Tesco's. 'Christ,' said Jake to himself, 'those windows are the same yellow as in Van Gogh's

sunflower painting!' Thus, ruminating on art and culture, did Jake pass the time.

Quite soon a sudden clap of thunder announced itself. 'Christ,' said Jake, 'that thunder sounds like the cannons of the 1812 Symphony!'.

He bitterly drew his anorak hood over his head, as raindrops like giant's tears fell on to the concrete wasteland. 'What am I doing here?' questioned Jake to himself. 'Why did I come?' he anguished. 'Where am I going?' he agonized. Just then a sudden rainbow appeared.

'Christ,' said Jake, 'that rainbow looks like....'

I had to stop there; I don't know where Jake came from, or where he's going either.

Friday   March 11th

Pandora Braithwaite is going out with Brain Box Henderson. I hope they'll both be very happy. Nigel says they spend all their time together talking about higher mathematics.

Did a bit of shouting outside the Youth Club doors tonight.

Rick Lemon pretended not to hear us, but I noticed that the vein in his temple was throbbing. Why don't my parents notice that I am turning into a yob?

Saturday   March 12th

Saw Danny Thompson, the white Rasta, outside the Chinese chip shop tonight. He asked me if I'd written any lyrics for the group yet. I said I'd go home straight away and write some. I was glad of an excuse to leave. I was tired of Barry Kent shoving his prawn balls down my trousers.

Sunday   March 13th
MOTHERING SUNDAY

Rat fink Lucas sent my mother a mother's day card signed 'Rosie'.

Grandma sent Stick Insect a card signed 'Brett'.

My mother sent Grandma Mole a card signed 'George'.

My father sent my Grandma Sugden a card signed 'Pauline'.

I didn't send the woman who gave birth to me a card this year. Interpersonal relationships in our family have gone completely to pot. This is what living with the shadow of the bomb does to you.

Monday   March 14th
COMMONWEALTH DAY

Barry Kent has been arrested for vandalizing hyacinths in the town hall square yesterday morning at 7 a.m.

He is pleading extenuating circumstances; they were to be a gift for his mother.

Tuesday   March 15th

Reasons for living	Reasons for not living
Things might get better	You die anyway
	Life is nothing but anguish
	There is too much cruelty in the world
	'O' levels in June
	My parents hate me
	I've lost Pandora
	Nobody leaves Barry Kent's gang alive.

Wednesday   March 16th

Elizabeth Sally Broadway keeps snatching my school scarf from round my neck and running away with it. forcing me to chase her. This is a sure sign that she is romantically interested in me. I can feel my hormones stirring for the first time in months.

Thursday   March 17th
ST PATRICK'S DAY

Elizabeth grabbed my executive brief case and sprinted across the sports field during the afternoon break.

I caught up with her in the shrubbery where we had a very enjoyable tussle which lasted five minutes and climaxed in me removing her glasses and hair pins.

She looked different unspectacled and with her hair down her back.

I said, 'But Elizabeth, you're beautiful.'

God knows what would have happened if the bell hadn't rung for the next lesson.

2 a.m. Can't sleep for the noise of Irish bagpipes leaking out of the O'Learys' house.

4 a.m. Just woken up by the sound of breaking glass.

6 a.m. A police car has just left the O'Learys' house taking Sean O'Leary with it. Sean looked quite cheerful, in fact he was singing a song about Forty Shades of Green.

Friday   March 18th

At last! My parents have noticed that I am out of control, and have banned me from going out after school.

Spent the evening re-reading *Black Beauty* for the fifth time.

Saturday   March 19th

I have written a letter to Barry Kent, resigning from the gang.

> Dear Baz,
> The crumblies have said I've got to stay in for a week. So I'll have to give hanging about with you and the lads a miss. Also Baz, they are forcing me to take my stinking exams in June, so I'd better resign from my place in the

gang and leave it open for somebody who needs it. I hope
your court case goes well. No hard feelings eh?
> Yours Fraternally,
> Brains

Sunday   March 20th
BRITISH SUMMER TIME BEGINS

8 p.m. Rained solidly all day.

10.30 p.m. How can it rain 'solidly'? What a strange mistress is
the English language.

Monday   March 21st

My parents have hardly spoken to me since Friday night. They
are too busy watching Rosie's manual dexterity develop.

Every time the kid grabs a plastic brick or shoves a rusk in her
mouth, she gets a round of applause.

Tuesday   March 22nd

I have decided to leave home.

Nobody will care. In fact my parents probably won't notice
that I've gone. I have given the Building Society one week's
notice of my intention to withdraw £50. There is no point in
losing interest unnecessarily.

Wednesday   March 23rd

I am making preparations to leave. I have already written my
goodbye letters.

> Pandora,
> I may be gone for some time.
> > Adrian

> Dear Mum and Dad,
> By the time you read this I will be far away. I know I am

breaking the law in running away before my 16th birthday, but, quite honestly, a life as a fugitive is preferable to my present miserable existence.

From your son,
A. Mole

Dear Bert,
I've taken your advice and gone off to see the world. You don't need me now that you've got all those wimpy volunteers hanging around you. But watch out, Bert, you are only popular because they think you are a character. Any day now they will find out that you are bad-tempered and foul-mouthed. I will send you a postcard from one of the corners of the world.

Adios Amigo,
P.S. Give my love to Sabre, and don't forget to give him his Bob Martins.

Dear Grandma,
Sorry to worry you but I have gone away for a bit. Please stop feuding with Mum and Dad. 'They know not what they do.' Rosie is lovely now, she would really like to see you.

Lots of love,
Adrian

Dear Mr Scruton,
By the time you read this I will be miles away from your scabby school. So don't bother sending the truant officer round. I intend to educate myself in the great school of life, and will never return.

A. Mole
P.S. Did you know that your nickname is 'Pop-Eye'? So-called because of your horrible manic sticking-out eyes. Everybody laughs at you behind your back, especially Mr Jones the PE teacher.
P.P.S. I think you should be ashamed of the fact that

Barry Kent *still can't read* after spending five years in your school.

Dearest Elizabeth,

I'm sorry that I have to leave just as our love was bursting into bud. But a boy has to do what a boy has to do.

Don't wait for me, Elizabeth. I may be gone for some time.

Yours with regrets and fondest memories,
Aidy Mole

Baz,

I've blown town. The pigs will be looking for me. Try and put 'em off the scent will you?
Brains

Nigel,

Good luck with being gay. I, too, am different from the herd; so I understand what it is like to be always out of step.

It's the ordinary people who will have to learn to accept us.

Any road up as we say in these parts.
Rock on Tommy!
Your old mate,
Aidy

Thursday March 24th

Five days to go. I am growing a beard.

I have borrowed my dead grandad's suitcase. Luckily he had the same initials as me. His name was Arnold.

Grandma thinks I am using it for a camping trip with the Youth Club. The truth would kill her.

Friday March 25th

I have started packing my case. A certain amount of

rationalization has had to take place regarding clean socks and underwear.

I will have to lower my standards and only change them every other day. No sign of the beard yet.

Saturday   March 26th

Courtney Elliot has been instructed by my father not to deliver any letters with a Sheffield postmark. But he brought one into the kitchen this morning saying, 'The Royal Mail has to get through, Mr Mole. We're like the Pony Express in that respect!'

My father ripped the letter into tiny pieces and foot-pedalled them into the bin.

Later on I retrieved the bits and stuck them together.

> . . . ole.
> . . . structed . . . client . . . ucas, civil action unless . . . Ros
> . . . ole . . . is his daughter. He wishes the aforesaid child to . . . Rosie Lucas.
>
> My client . . . blood test . . . under oath that . . . intercourse took . . . Pauline Mole . . . to hear from you . . .
>
> Yours Faithfully,
> Coveney, Tinker, Shulman, Solicitors

Sunday   March 27th

The crumblies spent three hours forcing Rosie to sit up on her own. But she kept sliding down the cushions and laughing. If she could talk I know what she would say, 'Stop interfering in my development, I'll do it when I'm ready!'

I pointed out that her back muscles are not strong enough yet, but the crumblies wouldn't listen. They said things like, 'Rosie is exceptionally forward,' and 'You were nowhere near as advanced as she is at five months!'

They will be sorry for these cutting words on Tuesday.

Monday   March 28th

An old American bloke called Ian MacGregor has been put in charge of the National Coal Board. It is a disgrace!

England has got loads of ruthless, out-of-work executives who would be delighted to be given the chance to close their own country's coalmines down. Mr Scargill is quite right to protest, he has my full support on this issue.

Packed my pyjamas and dressing gown.

It is RA day tomorrow. I have made out a list of vital equipment, clothing etc.

Roller skates
Shaving kit
3 jumpers
2 shirts
3 pairs trousers
5 pairs socks
Wellingtons
Doc Marten's
Plimsolls
Orange waterproof trousers
4 pairs underpants
4 vests
Diary
Survival handbook
Robinson Crusoe
*Down and Out in Paris and
    London*

*Penguin Medical
    Dictionary*
Junior aspirins
First aid box
Sleeping bag
Camping stove
Matches
6 tins beans
Spoon
Knife
Fork
Cruet
Serviettes
Transistor radio
The dog

Tuesday   March 29th

6 a.m.   Packed everything on list apart from the
          dog.
6.05   Took everything out.
6.10   Repacked.
6.15   Took everything out.

6.30	Repacked, but no good. Still can't get suitcase lid to shut. Decide not to take roller skates.
6.33	Ditto wellingtons.
6.35	Ditto camping stove.
6.37	Suitcase lid shuts.
6.39	Try to pick up suitcase. Can't.
6.40	Take out tins of beans.
6.44	Repack.
6.45	Get in a rage.
6.48	Take cruet and serviettes out.
6.55	Take Doc Marten's out of suitcase. Decide to wear them instead. Spend fifteen precious minutes in doing the sodding laces up.
7.10	Examine spots in bathroom.
7.13	Check farewell letters have got stamps on.
7.14	Pick suitcase up. Not bad. Not good.
7.15	Repack suitcase with half previous clothes.
7.19	Pick suitcase up. Better.
7.20	Remember sleeping bag. Try to pack it in suitcase.
7.21	Get in another rage.
7.22	Kick suitcase across bedroom floor.
7.22.30 secs.	Crumblies shout from their bedroom. Demanding to know what all the noise is about.
7.24	Make tea. Crumblies ask why I have got a tin opener in the breast pocket of my blazer. I lie and say that I've got Domestic Science for my first lesson.
7.31	Feed dog, make baby's breakfast slops.
7.36	Check Building Society account book.
7.37	Groom dog. Pack its personal possessions in suitcase: dog bowl, brush, vaccination certificate, worm tablets, lead, choke chain, 5 tins Chum, bag of Winalot.
7.42	Try to pick up suitcase, can't.

7.47	Decide to leave dog behind. Break the news to it.
7.49	Dog cries. Crumblies shout at it to be quiet.
7.50	Decide to take the dog after all.
8.00	Pack minimum amount of stuff in Adidas bag.
8.10	Hide Grandad's suitcase in wardrobe.
8.15	Say goodbye to Rosie.
8.20	Put dog on lead.
8.21	Wait until crumblies are distracted.
8.25	Leave house with dog.
8.30	Post farewell letters.
9.00	Draw £50 out of Building Society, and head North.

Wednesday   March 30th

3 p.m. Watford Gap Service Station. M1 Motorway.

My first mistake was waiting for a lift on the southern bound side of the motorway approach road.

My second mistake was bringing the dog.

7.31 Sheffield.

Got a lift in a pig delivery lorry. This is just my luck!

I had a very long conversation with the driver, which is a miracle really, because I couldn't hear a word he was saying over the noise of the engine. I am having to keep a low profile. Sheffield is rat fink Lucas's stamping ground.

Why doesn't my beard hurry up and grow?

9.30 p.m. Leeds.

Tuned into the Radio Four nine o'clock news. But no mention was made of my mysterious disappearance. I am writing this at the side of the canal. A man has just come up and asked me if I want to sell the dog. I was tempted but said no.

11.00 p.m. Rang home but the phone wasn't snatched up immediately like it is in the films about runaway children.

Another sign of their indifference.

Thursday   March 31st

1 a.m. The man who asked about the dog has just approached me and asked me if I want to sell *myself*. I said, 'No,' and told him my father was the Chief Constable of Wales.

He said, 'Why are you sleeping rough in Leeds?'

I told another lie, I said, 'My father has sent me on an initiative test. If I survive this he'll put me down for Hendon Police College.'

Why did I tell him such an elaborate lie? Why? I had to listen while he told me his many grievances against the police. I promised to pass them on to my father and copied his name and address into my diary:

> Stanley Gibbons,
> c/o Room 2,
> The Laurels Community Care Hostel,
> Paradise Cuttings,
> Leeds

He invited me to spend the night on his put-u-up, but I demurred, saying that my father was checking up on me via a long-distance telescope. He went then.

Friday   April 1st
GOOD FRIDAY. ALL FOOLS' DAY

10 a.m. Leeds. (A launderette.)

Thank God for launderettes, if they hadn't been invented I'd be dead of hydrophobia by now. Nowhere else is open.

It cost a *pound* to dry my sleeping bag. But I was so wet and cold that I didn't care at the time.

I am waiting for the dog to wake up. It was on guard duty last night protecting our respective bodies from Stanley Gibbons. I am sixteen tomorrow. But still no sign of a beard. Good Friday!

Saturday   April 2nd

Manchester Railway Station.
Got here by fish lorry. Pretended to be asleep in order to avoid driver's conversation.

10.31 a.m. I wonder what my mum and dad have bought me for my birthday. I hope they are not too worried. Perhaps I ought to ring them and convince them that I am well and happy.

12.15 p.m. We have been ordered out of the railway station café by a bad-tempered waitress. It's the stupid dog's fault. It kept going behind the counter and begging for bits of bacon.

Yet I bought it a bacon roll all to itself this morning.

3 p.m. Nobody has said 'Happy Birthday' to me.

3.05 p.m. I'm not well (I've got a cold) and I'm not happy. In fact I'm extremely unhappy.

5.30 p.m. Bought myself a birthday card. Inside I wrote:

> To our darling first-born child on his sixteenth birthday.
> With all the love it is possible to give,
> From your admiring and loving parents.
> PS. Come home son. Without you the house is devoid of life and laughter.

6.15 p.m. There was nothing about me on the six o'clock news.

7.30 p.m. Can't face another night in the open.

9 p.m. Park bench.

I have asked three policemen the time, but none of them have spotted me as a runaway. It's obvious that my description hasn't been circulated.

9.30 p.m. Just rang the police station, using a disguised voice. I said, 'Adrian Mole, a sixteen-year-old runaway, is in the vicinity of the Blood Transfusion Headquarters. His description is as follows: small for his age, slight build, mousey hair, disfigured skin. He is wearing a green school blazer. Orange waterproof trousers. A blue shirt. Balaclava helmet. Brown Doc Martens. With him is a mongrel dog, of the following description: medium height, hairy face, squint in left eye. Wearing a tartan collar and matching lead.'

The desk sergeant said, 'April Fool's Day was yesterday, sonny.'

10.00 p.m. Waited outside the Blood Transfusion place but there wasn't a policeman in sight. There is never one around when you need one.

11.39 p.m. I have walked past the police station twenty-four times, but none of the cretins in blue have given me a second glance.

11.45 p.m. I have just been turned away from an Indian Restaurant on the grounds that I wasn't wearing a tie, and was accompanied by a scruffy dog.

Sunday   April 3rd
EASTER SUNDAY

Still in Manchester. (St Ignatius's church porch.)

1 a.m. It is traditional for the homeless to sleep in church porches so why don't vicars make sure that their porches are more comfortable? It wouldn't kill them to provide a mattress, would it?

7.30 a.m. Got up at six. Had a wash in a bird bath. Read the inscriptions on the gravestones. Then went in search of a shop. Found one; bought two Cadbury's creme eggs. Ate one myself, gave the other to the dog. The poor thing was so hungry it ate the silver paper as well. I hope it won't be ill; I can't afford to pay for veterinary attention. I've only got £15.00 left.

Monday   April 4th

St Ignatius's church porch, Manchester.

6 a.m. For two days I have had the legal right to buy cigarettes, have sex, ride a moped, and live away from home. Yet, strangely, I don't want to do any of them now I'm able to.

Must stop. A woman with a kind face is coming through the gravestones.

9 a.m. I am in the vicar's wife's bed. She is a true Christian. She doesn't mind that I am an existentialist nihilist. She says I'll grow out of it. The dog is downstairs lying on top of the Aga.

10 a.m. Mrs Merryfield, the vicar's wife, has phoned my parents and asked them to come and fetch me. I asked Mrs Merryfield for my parents' reactions. She crumpled her kind face up in thought then said, 'Angry relief is the nearest I can get to it, dear!'

I haven't seen the vicar yet. He is having a lie-in because of being so busy yesterday. I hope he doesn't mind that a stranger is occupying his wife's bed.

12.30 p.m. The vicar has just gone. Thank God! What a bore! No wonder poor Mrs Merryfield sleeps apart from him. I expect that she is scared he'll talk about comparative religions in his sleep. I have just spent a week living rough. The last thing I want is a lecture on 'Monophysitism'.

2.30 p.m. The Reverend Merryfield brought my dinner in at 1.30, then gabbled on about 'Lamaism', the Tibetan religion, while my dinner got cold, and eventually congealed.

6 p.m. I notice my parents are not breaking their necks to get here. I wish they would hurry up. I've had 'Mithraism', 'Orphism' and 'Pentecostalism' up to here.

I'm all for a man having outside interests, but this is ridiculous.

Tuesday   April 5th

Bedroom. Home.
Well, there were no banners in the street, or crowds of people jostling to get a view as I got out of my father's car. Just my mother's haggard face at the lounge window, and Grandma's even haggarder one behind her.

My father doesn't talk when he's driving on motorways, so we had hardly said a word to each other, since leaving St Ignatius's vicarage. (And Reverend Merryfield saw to it that we didn't talk *at* the vicarage, what with his rabbiting on about Calvinism and Shakers. Mrs Merryfield tried to stop him: she said, 'Please be quiet, darling,' but it just set him off on Quietism.)

But my mother and Grandma said a great many things. Eventually I pleaded for mercy and went to bed and pulled the crispy white sheets over my head.

Wednesday   April 6th

Dr Grey has just left my bedside. He has diagnosed that I am suffering from a depressive illness brought on by worry. The treatment is bedrest, and no quarrelling in the family.

My parents are bowed down by guilt.

I can't rest for worrying about the letter I wrote to 'Pop-Eye' Scruton.

Thursday   April 7th

The dog is at the vet's, having the blisters on its paws treated. I got up for five minutes and looked out of my bedroom window

today. But there was nothing in the urban landscape to interest me, so I got back into bed.

I haven't opened my birthday presents yet.

Friday April 8th

Ate a Mars bar.

I can feel my physical strength returning, but my mental strength is still at rock bottom.

Saturday April 9th

10 a.m. I suffered a relapse so Dr Grey called round.

I lay back listlessly on the pillows and let him feel my pulse etc.

He muttered, 'Bloody Camille,' as he left the room.

Perhaps Camille is a drug that he's thinking of using on me.

12 noon. I asked my mother to draw the curtains against the sun.

Sunday April 10th

Lay all day with my head turned to the wall. Rosie was brought in to cheer me up, but her childish gibbering merely served to irritate so she was taken away.

Monday April 11th

Bert Baxter was carried up to my bedside, but his coarse exhortation, 'Get out of your pit, you idle bugger!' failed to stir me from my nihilistic thoughts.

Tuesday April 12th

Nigel has just left, after trying to arouse me by playing my favourite 'Toyah' tapes at a discreet volume.

I signalled that I would prefer both his and Toyah's absence.

Wednesday   April 13th

A sign that my parents are now frantic with worry about me;
Barry Kent was allowed into the house.

His inarticulate ramblings about the gang's activities failed
to interest or stimulate me, so he was led out of the darkened
room.

Thursday   April 14th

A consultant psychologist has been ordered.
Dr Grey has admitted his failure.

Friday   April 15th

Dr Donaldson has just left my bedside after listening to my
worries with grave attention.

When I'd sunk back on to my pillows he said, 'We'll take
them one by one.'

1. Nuclear war *is* a worry, but do something positive
   about your fear – join CND.
2. If you fail your 'O' levels you can retake them next
   year, or never take them – like the Queen.
3. Of course your parents love you. They didn't sleep
   during the time you were away.
4. You are *not* hideously ugly. You are a pleasant,
   average-looking boy.
5. Your sister's paternity problems are nothing to do
   with you, and there is nothing you can do to help.
6. I've never heard of a sixteen-year-old having their
   own poetry programme on Radio Four. You must set
   yourself realistic targets.
7. I will write to Mr Scruton ('Pop-Eye') and inform him
   that you were under great stress at the time you wrote
   the letter.
8. Pandora comes under the heading of insoluble
   problems.

Saturday   April 16th

Grandma came to my room at 8 a.m. this morning and ordered me out of bed!

She said, 'You've been pampered enough. Now pull yourself together, and go and shave that bum-fluff off your face!'

I weakly protested that I needed more time to find myself.

Grandma said, 'I need to wash those sheets so get out of bed!'

I said, 'But I'm angst-ridden.'

'Who wouldn't be after lying in a bed like a dying swan for a week!' was her callous reply.

My Grandma is a good honest woman, but her grasp of the intellectual niceties is minimal.

Spent the day on the settee sipping Lucozade.

Sunday   April 17th

Settee.

My parents are speaking to me in tones of forced gaiety. They are making pathetic attempts to bring me back into normal life by drawing my attention to items of interest on the television. 'Watch the news!' they brightly exclaimed. I did.

It was full of stories about murder, bombing, uncovered spies and disasters of rail, road and air. The only remotely cheerful item was about a man with no legs who'd walked from John O'Groats to Land's End. This proof of the cruelty of fate versus the magnificence of the human spirit reduced me to silent sobs into the Dralon cushions.

Monday   April 18th

The school holidays started today.

It is just my luck to be too ill to appreciate the break.

Tuesday   April 19th

> *Daffodils by A. Mole*
> While on my settee I lie
> From out of the corner of my eye

I spot a clump of Yellow Daffodils,
Bowing and shaking as a lorry goes by.
Brave green stalks supporting yellow bonnets.
Like the wife of a man who writes Love Sonnets.

Wednesday   April 20th

Ate four Shredded Wheat today.
  I can feel my strength slowly returning.

Thursday   April 21st

Pandora came to see me for ten minutes this afternoon.
  Brain Box Henderson stood at our gate, fiddling with his calculator. Perhaps he was trying to work out how much he loves Pandora.
  Well it won't be as much as me, Henderson. I can assure you of that fact!
  Pandora was wearing Monochromatic rags. She told me it was the latest fashion. She is coming back tomorrow.

Friday   April 22nd

I asked my mother if she would go to town and buy me three tee-shirts. One black, one white and one grey.
  When she came back I set about the tee-shirts with a pair of scissors. Grandma took this to be a symptom of my escalating madness. I tried to explain that it was how we in the teenage sub-culture are dressing now. But she couldn't take it in.
  When my father saw me wearing rags he went pale and almost said something. But my mother whispered, 'Not now, George, don't send him off again!'
  Pandora came round at 5 p.m. By the end of *John Craven's News Round* we were in each other's arms. Our rags entangled, our lips on fire.

Saturday   April 23rd

Pandora went round to Brain Box Henderson's house to break

the news, but he was out buying floppy discs, so she left a message on his word processor. Getting Pandora back from him is a triumph of Art over Technology.

Sunday April 24th

I am reading *Kingsley, The Life, Letters and Diaries of Kingsley Martin*, by C. H. Rolf. Strangely, it doesn't mention that he wrote *Lucky Jim*.

Monday April 25th

Went for a walk with Pandora and Rosie.

(That is to say Pandora and I walked, but lucky Rosie was pushed in her pram.) We called in to see Bert. He was dead pleased to see us. He has been deserted by his voluntary helpers, and hadn't got any Woodbines in the house. He smelt rotten so we stripped him off and put him in the bath. (Bert insisted that Pandora put a flannel over her eyes for this part of the operation.) Then I washed his bit of remaining hair and gave him a good scrub down, while Pandora took Rosie and Sabre and went to Mr Patel's for Woodbines.

When Pandora came back we lifted Bert out of the bath. (Pandora promised to keep her eyes shut) and I dried him and put him into clean pyjamas. He looked lovely with his white hair all fluffy and sticking out at the back of his head. If I'd been a householder I would have invited him to stay there and then. Bert needs twenty-four-hour round-the-clock care, by people who love him.

The problem is that very few people, apart from Mother Theresa and a few nuns, could put up with Bert for more than a couple of days.

I asked him if there was any chance of him turning Catholic, he said, 'About as much chance as there is of Mrs Thatcher turning into a woman!'

On the way home we played a good game. We pretended we were married and that Rosie was our baby. Pandora tired of the game before I did but not before several people had been fooled.

Tuesday   April 26th

The dog had an unfortunate accident on the kitchen floor this morning. Unfortunate for me, that is, because I had to clear it up. Knowing its use for such emergencies, I grabbed this week's copy of *The Sunday Times*, and made the thrilling discovery that HITLER'S DIARIES HAVE BEEN FOUND! I quote, 'After being hidden in a German hayloft for nearly forty years, *The Sunday Times* today tells the full story of this historic discovery!' I read on avidly. And to think I nearly used such a revelatory article to wipe up a piece of dog crap!

Wednesday   April 27th

Is there no trust left in the world?

The Hitler Diaries are being subjected to meticulous tests by scientists. Why can't they take *The Sunday Times*' word for it that the diaries are genuine? Even a sceptic like me knows that *The Sunday Times* wouldn't risk its reputation if there was the faintest chance that the diaries were a forgery.

Thursday   April 28th

Herr Wolf-Rudiger Hess, son of Rudolph Hess (Hitler's Deputy Maniac) has said that the Hitler Diaries are genuine. So there, Pandora! Incidentally, Rudolph Hess is eighty-nine. The same age as Bert Baxter.

Friday   April 29th

My father took me and Rosie to the bank. To help him get a bank loan. Mr Niggard, the Bank Manager, looked at my rags in a pitying way. Then said, 'Why do you require this loan, Mr Mole? A car, a house extension or clothes for the children perhaps?'

My father said, 'No. I can't afford to *buy* anything. I just want to feel some money in my hand again.'

But, after hearing that my parents were both out of work and

on the Social, Mr Niggard refused the loan, saying: 'I am saving you from yourself. You will thank me one day.'

My father said, 'No I won't, I'm taking my overdraft elsewhere.'

Saturday   April 30th

My mother has decided that sugar is the cause of all the evil in the world, and has banned it from the house.

She smoked two cigarettes while she informed me of her decision.

Sunday   May 1st

I overheard my father say, 'Well it looks like the North Sea for me, Pauline.'

I ran into the kitchen and said, 'Don't do it, Dad. The economy is bound to pick up!'

My father looked puzzled. Perhaps he was surprised to hear such an emotional outburst from me.

I was surprised myself.

Monday   May 2nd
BANK HOLIDAY

Lord Dacre has vouched for the Hitler Diaries' authenticity.

So Pandora owes me £1.50 in a lost bet. Ha! Ha! Ha!

Tuesday   May 3rd
BACK TO SCHOOL

Quite a few changes have taken place since I was last at school. Mr Jones the PE teacher has got the sack, and Mr Lambert has married Ms Fossington-Gore; he is now called Mr Lambert-Fossington-Gore. She is called Ms Fossington-Gore-Lambert.

Mr Scruton is on sick leave, suffering from a breakdown due to compiling the timetable, so Podgy Pickles the Deputy head

has taken over his functions. The new regime is a bit more relaxed, though not yet liberal enough to enable me to wear my rags to school.

We spent the first day back being taught how to revise for the dreaded 'O' levels.

6 p.m. Started revising English, Biology and Geography.

7 p.m. Decided to concentrate on one subject at a time. Chose English.

8 p.m. Finished revising when Bert Baxter phoned and requested my help. His toilet is blocked again.

Wednesday　May 4th

Got a letter from L. S. Caton – the man who recognizes my writing talent. The postmark said '*New York.*'

> Dear Adrian Mole,
> Thank you for sending me the first page of your novel, *Longing for Wolverhampton*. I am sure that any publishing house worth its salt would jump at the chance to publish such a promising piece of work.
>   For a small consideration (shall we say, $100), I would be pleased to promote your book.
>   Make your cheque out to: L. S. Caton Ltd.
> and send it to me, c/o The Dixon Motel,
> 1,599 Block 19,
> NY State
> USA

My father refused to give me the money after reading the first page of *Longing for Wolverhampton*! He said, 'I've read some rubbish in my life, but this....'

Thursday　May 5th

My father has gone for an interview to be a roustabout on an oil rig in the North Sea.

My father a roustabout!

It is nearly as good as having a cowboy for a father. I hope he gets the job. He will be away one fortnight in two.

Friday   May 6th

Yet another disenchantment.

The Hitler Diaries are a hoax. I have paid Pandora £1.50.

I am dead disappointed, I was looking forward to reading about what maniacs eat for breakfast, and how they behave in private.

Saturday   May 7th

Spent all day revising with Pandora in her mother's study.

Our house is intolerable because my father is beside himself with grief at being turned down by the oil rig firm.

I *told him* it was a bit premature to buy the check shirts and jeans, before he'd been notified that he'd got the job, but he wouldn't listen.

Now he owes Grandma £38.39.

Sunday   May 8th

The Sunday Times has printed a grovelling apology to its readers, and ex-readers.

I will save today's edition and use it to clean up any future dog crap. Adrian Mole does not like being made to look a fool.

Especially in front of the future Mrs Adrian Mole, *née* Pandora Braithwaite.

Monday   May 9th

Mrs Thatcher has called a General Election for June 9th!

How selfish can you get?

Doesn't she know that the May and early June period is supposed to be kept quiet, while teenagers revise for their exams? How can we study when loudspeakers are blaring out

lying promises, day and night and canvassers are continually knocking on the door, reminding floating voters that it's 'make your mind up' time? It's all right for her to announce she is going to the country, but some of us can't afford that luxury.

Tuesday   May 10th

I keep getting anxiety attacks every time I think about the exams.

I know I'm going to fail.

My overriding problem is that I'm *too* intellectual: I am constantly thinking about things, like: was God married? and: if Hell is other people, is Heaven empty?

These thoughts overload my brain, causing me to forget *facts*. Such as: the average rainfall in the average Equatorial Forest and other boring stuff.

Wednesday   May 11th

Grandma has given me some brain pills as a revision aid.

They are concocted from a disgusting part of a bull. She said, 'Your dead Grandad swore by them.' I swallowed two this morning but by the afternoon I still couldn't remember the capital of British Honduras.

I swore by them as well.

Thursday   May 12th

I thought my parents had given up the idea of moving house, but no! My mother struck terror into my heart and bowels at breakfast time by announcing that after the exams, we are going to sell our house and move to a desolate area of Wales! She said, 'I want to give us a chance of surviving a nuclear attack.'

I have written to the Council asking to be put on the waiting list.

I requested a two-bedroom flat facing south, with balcony and a working lift.

Friday   May 13th

My mother and father are having to negotiate a new Marriage
Contract. I'm not surprised; my father hates Wales. He even
complains when it is shown on television.

My mother has borrowed ominous books from the library:
The Treatment of Radiation Burns; *Bee-Keeping, an Introduction*;
and *Living without Men – A Practical Guide*.

Saturday   May 14th

10 a.m. A bloke in a blue-and-white pin-striped suit, blue shirt,
blue tie, blue rosette, has just knocked at the door. Thrust his
hand out, said, 'Julian Pryce-Pinfold: your Conservative
candidate, 'I trust I have your vote!'

I was quite pleased to be taken for eighteen. But I said, 'No,
you are planning to exterminate the working class!'

Pryce-Pinfold laughed like a horse and said, 'I say, don't go
over the top old chap, we're just trying to trim 'em down a bit!'

He left his poster so I drew devil's horns on his head and
wrote '666' on his forehead, and put it up in the lounge
window.

Sunday   May 15th

A bloke in a grey suit, white shirt, and red tie, has just disturbed
my Biology revision by knocking on the door and announcing
that he is the Labour Candidate. He said, 'I'm Dave Blakely
and I'm going to get Britain back to work!'

My father asked him if there were any jobs going in the
Labour Party headquarters. (A sign of his desperation.)

Dave Blakely said that he had never been to the
headquarters so he didn't know.

He said, 'I disagree with official Labour policy.'

My mother harangued him about nuclear disarmament and
criticized the Labour Party's record on housing, education and
trade union co-operation.

Dave Blakely said, 'I suppose you're a Tory are you madam?'

My mother snapped: 'Certainly not, I have voted Labour all my life!'

Monday   May 16th

A blonde man in a blazer, with a regimental badge stood outside the school gates handing out election leaflets this afternoon. I read mine on the way home. The man is called Duncan McIntosh and his party is called 'The Send 'Em Back Where They Come From Party.' Its policy is the compulsory repatriation of: black people, brown people, yellow people, tinged people, Jewish, Irish, Welsh, Scottish, Celtic and all those who have Norman blood.

In fact only those who can prove to be pure-bred flaxen-haired Saxons are to be allowed to live in this country.

My mother has worked out that if he came to power the population of Great Britain would be reduced to one.

Tuesday   May 17th

Barry Kent has threatened Duncan McIntosh with grievous bodily harm unless he keeps away from our school.

He has joined 'Rock against Racism' (Barry Kent not Duncan McIntosh).

Wednesday   May 18th

The SDP candidate (green suit, orange shirt, neutral tie, nervous smile) has just left our house on the verge of tears, after my mother refused to let her kiss Rosie.

Thursday   May 19th

I was shown a blurred picture of a broken-down cottage this morning, and asked if I would like to live there.

I replied in the negative.

My mother said, 'It sounds perfect. It's two miles from the nearest shop and fifty-five miles from the nearest American Air

Base! Wouldn't you like to get up in the morning and feed the chickens, Adrian?'

I replied, 'I hate chickens. Their nasty beaks and cruel eyes absolutely repel me.'

Friday   May 20th

Scruton has retired on the grounds of ill health (gone barmy) and Podgy Pickles has got his name screwed on to the Headmaster's door.

I have never been taught by Podgy, but by all accounts he is a nice bloke who talks about his family, and informs his class when he is thinking of buying a new car.

He took assembly this morning. He had dried egg yolk running down the length of his tie. I know because I was standing next to him. He had called me up to the stage to address the school on 'Why I think school uniform should be abolished!' I spoke from the heart, citing my parents' poverty, and bringing tears to the eyes of Ms Fossington-Gore-Lambert.

Saturday   May 21st

My father ordered three politicians out of the front garden this morning. He said, 'My son is upstairs studying for a better future, and your constant clamouring for attention is distracting him!'

Actually I was measuring my thing at the time, but their noise *was* distracting. I kept losing my place on the tape-measure.

Sunday   May 22nd

Rosie started crawling at 5 p.m.

My parents gave her a standing ovation.

Monday   May 23rd

My English essay 'Despair' was read out to the class.

Everyone looked dead miserable at the end. It is a story about

a hamster with an incurable disease. I asked Mr Lambert-Fossington-Gore if it was of sufficient quality to send to the BBC.

He laughed and said, 'Only the Natural History Unit at Bristol.'

I have taken his advice and sent it.

Tuesday   May 24th

I have hung a notice on my door. It says: 'ATTENTION! NO ONE ALLOWED PAST THIS POINT!'

I am sick of having my privacy invaded.

Wednesday   May 25th

No one came into my room to wake me up. So I was late for school and when I got home my dirty washing was still on the floor and my curtains were drawn.

Thursday   May 26th

My racing bike has been stolen from out of the back garden.

The prime suspects are the dustmen. They have never forgiven us for having maggots in our dustbin last summer.

Friday   May 27th

Followed the dustbin men up our road and tried to overhear any suspicious conversation, but they were only talking about Len Fairclough.

One of them warned me to keep away from the mangling machinery at the back. Was this a hint of the violence to come, if I voice my suspicions to the police?

Saturday   May 28th

Nigel brought my bike back today.

He intended to run away on it to avoid his 'O' levels, but decided not to after his father bought him a set of video cassette

study aids. We are the only family in our street who haven't got a video, so there's no point in asking my parents for similar technological help. I will just have to rely on my brain.

Sunday   May 29th

Stayed in bed all day revising.

Bert Baxter phoned three times but each time I told my parents to tell him that I was out of town.

The third time he rang, my mother said, 'Was it anything important, Bert?' Bert said, 'Not really, I just wanted to tell him that I think I'm ninety today.'

Felt such a rat fink that I pretended to return from out of town. I went to see him and gave him ninety gentle bumps (although I'm sure he's due at least one more).

It seemed to do him good.

Monday   May 30th

Wrote some lyrics for Danny Thomson's reggae band.

> *Hear what he saying by A. Mole*
> Sisters and Brothers listen to Jah,
> Hear his words from near and far,
> Haile Selassie he sit on the throne.
> Hear what he saying, Hear what he saying. (*Repeated 10 times.*)
> JAH! JAH! JAH!
>
> Rise up and follow Selassie, the king.
> A new tomorrow to you he will bring. (*Repeat.*)
> E-thi-o-pi-a,
> He'll bring new hope to ya.
> Hear what he saying. Hear what he saying. (*Repeated 20 times.*)

I gave it to Danny Thomson in Geography.

He read it, and said, 'Not bad, for a honky!'

What a cheek, he's twice as white as I am!

Pandora's mother has decided that the dynamics in our family are beyond her. She has recommended that we go to see a family therapist.

Tuesday   May 31st

Got a letter from Johnny Tydeman.

I can't remember any of the references it contains. Did I really write a poem called 'Autumn Renewal'?

I must have written it while the balance of my mind was disturbed in April.

> British Broadcasting Corporation
> 30th May

Dear Adrian Mole,

I do not think I will call you 'Aidy' and I think that it is a little premature in our correspondence for you to call me 'Johnny'. In fact I am never known as 'Johnny', only as 'John.' I do not wish to sound like a stuffy old grown-up, but when you are writing to people officially it is polite for one of your years to address them formally – though I do not mind, at this stage in our correspondence, your addressing me as 'Dear John Tydeman.' But 'Johnny', no! I do have several nicknames by which my friends know me but I am not going to reveal them to you. They relate largely to my surname rather than my Christian name.

Your last letter was altogether rather peculiar. Had you been at your parents' cocktail cabinet by any chance? Or had you drained the dregs of the previous night's vino? I do hope you had not tried glue-sniffing again. At least I am very pleased to hear that you have decided not to kill yourself this year. It would be a shocking waste. A poet can only die young when he has written a number of successful poems – *vide*: Keats, Shelley, Chatterton and Co. Most poets write drivel in their old age – *vide*: Wordsworth and quite a lot of Tennyson. I am sure your

mother would miss you very much, so it is best that you remain alive.

Perhaps under the influence of something or other, your grammar seems to have gone to pot, eg: 'I have wrote some.' But your poem 'Autumn Renewal' certainly has its moments. I like the pun about chaps. A bit rude though. 'Dandeline' (sic – not 'sick'!) is actually spelt 'dandelion' so you can't make it rhyme with 'decline' nor 'Vaseline' – try as you will.

Do not worry about our files. They will be shredded before the KGB can get to them. Your secrets are safe in Ware and Caversham.

With my best wishes and continued good luck with your writing efforts.

Yours,
John Tydeman

Wednesday   June 1st

This will be my last entry; until the exams are over.

Courtney Elliot is coming round to give me last-minute coaching; must stop, his taxi has just drawn up outside.

Thursday   June 2nd

My parents went to see a family therapist last night. During their absence Pandora and I indulged in extremely heavy petting; so heavy that I felt a weight fall from me.

If I don't pass my exams it won't matter.

I have known what it is to have the love of a good woman.

THE SECRET DIARY OF ADRIAN MOLE AGED 13¾

THURSDAY JANUARY 1st

These are my new year's resolutions:

1   *I will help the blind across the road.*
2   *I will hang my trousers up.*
3   *I will put the sleeves back on my records.*
4   *I will not start smoking.*
5   *I will stop squeezing my spots.*
6   *I will be kind to the dog.*
7   *I will help the poor and ignorant.*
8   *After hearing the disgusting noises from down stairs last night, I have also vowed never to drink alcohol.*

Plagued by spots, bullied, torn apart by family rows and shunned by the BBC who refuse his poems, Adrian Mole retreats into his own world.

"I wish I'd read this first." Samuel Pepys.

The book that almost changed a generation.

Sue Townsend

TRUE CONFESSIONS OF ADRIAN MOLE

Adrian Mole: 16¾ to 21 and four months.

Adrian Mole has grown up. He is no longer the callow youth
that pined so ardently for Pandora but has turned his
attention to higher things . . .

Thursday July 17th
Miss Sarah Ferguson was born to be the wife of Adrian Mole. I have
written to tell her so, and to implore her to change her mind before 23rd
July. As yet I have received no reply. She must be agonising over her
decision: 'Riches, glamour and publicity with Prince Andrew, or
poverty, introspection and listening to poetry with Adrian Mole' – not
an easy choice.

It is typical of Adrian's generosity that he has allowed some
space for two other entertaining if less distinguished writers.
One of them is Sue Townsend with some astute and light-
hearted lines of her own: the other is the unknown Margaret
Hilda Roberts, a particularly precocious adolescent from
Grantham with designs on the world . . .

A selected list of titles available from Mammoth

While every effort is made to keep prices low, it is sometimes necessary to increase prices at short notice. Mandarin Paperbacks reserves the right to show new retail prices on covers which may differ from those previously advertised in the text or elsewhere.

The prices shown below were correct at the time of going to press.

☐	7497 0095 5	**Among Friends**	Caroline B Cooney £2.99
☐	7497 0145 5	**Through the Nightsea Wall**	Otto Coontz £2.99
☐	7497 0582 5	**The Promise**	Monica Hughes £2.99
☐	7497 0171 4	**One Step Beyond**	Pete Johnson £2.50
☐	7497 0281 8	**The Homeward Bounders**	Diana Wynne Jones £2.99
☐	7497 0312 1	**The Changeover**	Margaret Mahy £2.99
☐	7497 0473 X	**Shellshock**	Anthony Masters £2.99
☐	7497 0323 7	**Silver**	Norma Fox Mazer £3.50
☐	7497 0325 3	**The Girl of his Dreams**	Harry Mazer £2.99
☐	7497 0280 X	**Beyond the Labyrinth**	Gillian Rubinstein £2.50
☐	7497 0558 2	**Frankie's Story**	Catherine Sefton £2.50
☐	7497 0009 2	**Secret Diary of Adrian Mole**	Sue Townsend £2.99
☐	7497 0333 4	**Plague 99**	Jean Ure £2.99
☐	7497 0147 1	**A Walk on the Wild Side**	Robert Westall £2.99

All these books are available at your bookshop or newsagent, or can be ordered direct from the publisher. Just tick the titles you want and fill in the form below.

Cash Sales Department, PO Box 5, Rushden, Northants NN10 6YX.
Fax: 0933 410321 : Phone 0933 410511.

Please send cheque, payable to 'Reed Book Services Ltd.', or postal order for purchase price quoted and allow the following for postage and packing:

£1.00 for the first book, 50p for the second; **FREE POSTAGE AND PACKING FOR THREE BOOKS OR MORE PER ORDER.**

NAME (Block letters) ....

ADDRESS ....

....

☐ I enclose my remittance for ....

☐ I wish to pay by Access/Visa Card Number

Expiry Date

Signature ....

Please quote our reference: MAND